Mountain Glory

Mountain Glory

The Brimstone Mountain Series
By
Margaret Bowling

ISBN: 978-1500297329

This is a work of fiction. Names, characters and
incidents either are the product of the author's
imagination or used fictitiously.

Published 2014

Cover photograph and design by –lyn Neilans

G

G J Publishing
515 Cimarron Circle Ste 323
Loudon Tennessee 37774
865-458-1355 / 865-567-5394
Booksbyneilans@aol.com

To order more copies, go to:
www.neilans.com

*Dedicated to the memory of
my cousin and my friend*
Jackie Sue Bruner Regan

Contents

Introduction

My hard-working and rugged ancestors were born and raised in East Tennessee, and they left a rich history and heritage that remained undiscovered for generations.

My great-grandfather, William Wilson, left his home to study law in Alabama, but later returned to his Tennessee roots. Scott County was to be his home for the rest of his days, and was to be the birthplace of my grandmother and my father.

When I first visited Scott County in 1970, I immediately knew it was a place that meant something special to me. My forebears worked hard to survive; they loved these mountains, and through learning about their lives I learned what family really means.

I loved the mountains and the creeks, cold and downward flowing, which brought life to the people and the wildlife that populated the forests and contributed to the survival of my ancestors.

I was in awe as I gazed upon the tombstones of those individuals who made the mountains their home. Familiar names were cut into the sandstone, recording the history of my roots.

Herein, then, is the story of those courageous pioneers who were responsible for me and my kin, and I pay tribute to them with gratitude.

Will and Lydia Wilson

Will and Lydia Wilson sat on the porch watching the sun set behind the trees and enjoying a welcome cool breeze. Will mused, "We have been happy here in the mountains, haven't we? Our Dent and Martha are grown and the boys George and John are growing into handsome teenagers. I think we have done well. Caroline will be out of school and wanting to go off to Knoxville pretty soon. Thank goodness we still have Mike and Nancy. I can't imagine the house without children!"

"Yes, we have been blessed. Do you ever regret leaving your good job in Alabama?"

"No. I am content with my land and my family. God has been good to us."

Earl and Evie Brown

Will Wilson had just come out onto his porch when he saw his old friend, Earl Brown, driving down the lane to his house. He lit his pipe, sat down in his old rocker, and waited.

"I have wonderful news, Will."

"Well, let's hear it!"

"Judge Lewellen has told me that there is a child at his house, and there's a chance that Evie and I can adopt her."

"That is good news!"

"Her name is Amy and her parents drowned in Buffalo Creek on Brimstone Mountain. She's a ward of the Scott County Court. We will go to the judge's house tomorrow to meet her."

Lydia overheard the conversation from inside the house, and came out to join them on the porch. "That's wonderful, Earl! Evie will be so happy!"

"You know how long Evie and I have wanted a child. This looks like our dream may come true."

Will and Lydia were fond of all their neighbors, but especially fond of Earl and Evie, who had been among the first to befriend them when they had first come to Norma.

The young couple lived in a small house across the street from Luther Harness' general store/post office. Earl made beds, chests, cabinets, and other necessary pieces of furniture in his woodworking shop next door for the townspeople.

Evie had a small vegetable garden in the back near the barn. There she enjoyed many happy and worthwhile hours. A large sheltering oak made a delightful place for her to rest and enjoy her flowers after long days of hoeing and planting. Even though their days were busy, they longed for children.

The next day, while Rachel Lewellen was preparing dinner, little Amy was playing with a kitten on the floor. Rachel tried to talk to the child but Amy would not talk to anyone but Joel. When she heard him coming she ran to the door at once, but she saw he was not alone and she shrank back and picked up the kitten once more.

Joel came in with a big smile for the girl. "How is my little sweetheart today?" he asked, adding, "this is Mr. And Mrs. Brown, Amy. They have come for dinner."

Rachel served the food and the grownups talked, but Amy ate very little and said nothing.

After dinner Judge Lewellen spoke to Earl and Evie alone.

Earl said, "She is adorable."

Evie added, "Oh, yes! We want her as soon as possible."

Earl got right to the point: "How soon can we sign the papers?"

"Go to the courthouse and talk to the clerk. He's expecting you and will start the paperwork immediately."

At home Evie was so excited she had trouble sleeping. She wanted this child so much. She asked Earl to help her prepare a back room for Amy so it would be all ready for her. For days they prepared the little bedroom. Evie made a pink spread for the bed and a pink cover for the night table; she set a small rocker near the window while Earl washed windows and hung new curtains. Finally, Evie was tired but content. At last her dream was coming true.

When the time came for them to go get Amy, Evie was almost ill with nerves.

"I do hope she likes us, Earl. She needs us as much as we need her."

While Earl and Evie were busy at their home, Rachel Lewellen was preparing dinner in her kitchen and talking to Amy at the same time. "Mrs. Brown prays every night for God to send her a little girl of her very own. Perhaps you'd like to be that girl?"

"I don't think so."

"I know, but she's so lonely."

"But why can't I stay here with Uncle Joel and you?"

"Because we have to have the little room ready for the next child who comes and has no one to love them."

Amy got very quiet, and thought about that for a few minutes.

When Joel came home for dinner, once again Earl and Evie were with him. Amy rushed into Joel's arms. After the meal, Evie asked Amy to walk with her in the Lewellen's rose garden. They sat together on a bench, and Evie asked, "Aren't these flowers pretty? Do you like them?"

Amy nodded.

"If you like, we can have Earl plant some flowers for you just like these at our house. And I have a room all fixed up for you. There is even a doll waiting on the pillow. Do you think you would like to come and just try the room out?"

Amy nodded timidly.

Evie smiled and said, "I hope you will like it."

The newly formed little family left after Joel and Rachel hugged Amy goodbye, and told her to come and visit whenever she wanted.

At first the little girl was shy with her new parents. They had named her Amy Evelyn Brown. Both Earl and Evie were understanding and kind.

One night Evie was awakened by Amy crying softly and ran to her room. "What's wrong, Honey? Did you have a bad dream?"

"Yes," sobbed Amy, "I saw Mommy and Daddy in the water again."

"Oh, poor baby," Evie said, and got into bed with Amy and held her until she slept soundly again.

Back in her own bed, Evie told Earl about Amy's bad dream.

"I feel so sorry for her. She really has been through a bad tragedy."

Many nights after that, Amy had nightmares about her parents. Evie talked to her friend, Mollie Creech, about it. As usual, Mollie had good advice. "She's grieving, Evie. I think you should get her a cat or dog. Sometimes that works well."

So Evie took Amy to visit the Wilsons. Caroline Wilson showed the little girl the new kittens in the barn, and Lydia told her she could have her choice. Amy picked out a white one with black spots, which she immediately named *Fluffy*. They visited for a while, and then Evie drove the little buggy home with Amy holding her new playmate. Soon the little girl was completely settled in, and suffered no more sleepless nights.

Dent Wilson

Dent dreaded telling his parents that he wanted to leave. As he pitched hay into the stalls he went over the conversation in his mind. He felt sure his father would be all right with the plan, but he couldn't be so sure about his mother. When his father's hired hand Kirby Lee came into the barn, Dent said, "You've been here for a while. What do you think Papa would say if I told him I wanted to go off on my own and find work?" Kirby replied thoughtfully, "I don't know, but I've heard him tell of leaving the mountain himself to go study law in Alabama when he was young. He might understand."

Dent sighed. "I sure hope so."

Dent had saved every penny he could from the sale of animal pelts and herbs he had gathered in the woods. He had sold everything directly to the trader instead of letting Luther Harness, at the general store, sell them for him. That way he kept more of his income for himself.

He finally decided he had enough for a start and had a talk with his parents, convincing them that he needed to get away for a couple of days to take a short trip to Knoxville.

He packed only a small satchel, placing inside some small samples of his wood carvings and a change of clothes. The night before he was to leave on the early train from Bean Station, he found he was too excited to sleep. He rose and walked outside, where he saw his father also walking in the moonlight. He smiled and joined him.

"I guess you couldn't sleep either!"

"I kept remembering when I packed and left," said Will. "I left my mother crying. For you it will be different. Lydia told me she did not want you to remember her in tears but with hope for your future."

"I'll remember that, Papa. I want her to be happy for me."

The train was sooty and very warm for so early in the day.

Dent watched the countryside flash by, and talked with all who would start a conversation. He gave out little information of his own for he had heard wild stories of things that had happened to travelers. He had pinned his money into his undershirt - all except what he would need the first day. He trusted no one but watched everything from his seat. Soon the coach arrived in Knoxville. His new adventure had begun!

The city streets were crowded. Dent noticed the way others were dressed, and felt self-conscious, and that his own clothes were very out of style. He had to ask around about a place to stay, where the furniture stores were, the historic spots, and the Tennessee River.

He knew from his school days that Knoxville had played an important part in the beginning of the state, and he saw as much as he could before he went to a rooming house for a meal and a hot bath.

The next morning he entered a large store called Holman's Furniture. Mr. Holman showed him the latest styles and some of his better selections.

"Your pieces are much more advanced than any we have in the mountains," Dent said. "Here are some examples of the timber in Scott County." He pulled out several carvings of birds and animals he had brought with him.

"These are very good. I would like to buy some of them to put on display to show the native woods," Mr. Holman said.

They agreed on a price and Dent was very happy that someone appreciated his work.

"There's a carpenter in New River you may want to meet, a Mr. Chapman. He makes the pieces for his shop and you would probably get work there with him. I can give you a reference. He is a good friend of mine."

"I really appreciate that, and thanks for everything."

Dent returned to his parents' farm full of optimism and cheer.

Everyone waved from the porch as Dent drove off with his father to the depot to go to New River to see the furniture store owner recommended by the fellow in Knoxville. This time he took two suitcases for he meant to stay. He had written to Mr. Chapman and was confident he could find work there, or close by. He was excited to start his new life in the work he liked to do. Dent met John Chapman and liked him on sight. He also met the store owner's daughter, Delores, who kept house for her father. She was nineteen and petite, with black curly hair and a sunny smile.

Mr. Chapman hired Dent immediately.

"You can start right away. Would you be interested in living here in our home? That way you won't have to spend any extra money on a rooming house."

Dent proved to be an efficient employee and learned much from John. "You're coming along fine," His employer told him. "You know how to deal with people and set up displays as well as managing the business end."

Delores worked at the front of the store a few hours a week so John could continue working with his new pieces. She suggested that her father should build a new front for the building, and helped him design the new entry and put up a new sign.

"You're just about the smartest girl I've ever met," Dent told her. He didn't tell her that he also thought she was the prettiest.

Dent wrote long letters home to his parents and his younger sister. Martha answered all of his letters at once and shared her longing to leave the family home, too.

He went home whenever he could to take gifts and visit. Everyone, from his former school mates to his father's friends and neighbors, was always eager to hear of his success.

Kirby Lee

When Kirby came into the kitchen the morning was fresh and dewy; silver and rose-colored streaks brightened the eastern sky. Stella Lawson, the young woman who had come to live with them to help Lydia with the household chores, had browned the biscuits, and the kitchen smelled deliciously of sausage and fried eggs. He found Will having breakfast, so he joined him at the table and they began planning their day.

Kirby drank his second cup of strong coffee, then rose from the table.

"I'll go milk, then I'll join you in the field."

Kirby always liked the early mornings in the mountains. He was refreshed from restful sleep, and felt great. While he milked the cow, leaning his head against her warm flank, he thought about his friend, Paul Redmond, who had come with him to Scott County to work on the Wilson farm several years earlier.

Paul had married Stella's sister Kathy and now was living on the Lawson homestead with her widowed father, Sam. Kirby missed Paul's companionship.

Although Kirby was happy for his friends, thinking of them reminded him of his own sweet Molly, waiting for him back in Roane County. Suddenly he was a little homesick for his old home.

Later that week when Will was hoeing corn on a sloping field, and had just paused to rest his back, he saw Kirby coming toward him.

"Will, I need to talk to you," he said. "I have a letter from my sister. She says my father is very ill and asks me to come home. She says my mother wants me there, too."

"I'm sorry to hear that. When do you want to leave?"

"Just as soon as I can."

"Go on to the house and tell Lydia. Start packing. I'll be there as soon as I finish this row."

Will sighed. First Paul Redmond had left, then Dent, and now Kirby was going, too. He would need to find a replacement farm hand - and soon.

Will drove Kirby to the station. "I'll write you as soon as I can, Will. I just don't know how long I'll have to be gone. I wish you luck in finding more help."

Charlie Tarwater

Earl and Evie Brown were so happy. Evie delighted in sewing little dresses for Amy, and sunbonnets, too, to protect her delicate skin from the sun. Their little girl's musical laughter rang throughout their home, and they felt very blessed.

Today Earl was especially elated. Lately his business had picked up and he felt ready to expand the shop; then he learned of some acreage available for purchase on the west side of Norma.

Earl examined the piece of land at length, finding that it had a spring and lots of hardwood trees that would be perfect for building both a larger shop and a new home for his little family.

He signed the papers for the purchase, obtained a small loan from the bank, and immediately began working on plans for a small shelter which he could use while he was felling trees for the new structures. He worked in his shop filling orders for shelves and bedsteads and the many useful things his mountain neighbors needed, and also spent long hours at the new property.

"You look exhausted, Earl," Evie sympathized.

"Yes, I suppose I am tired; but I feel very content, too," he smiled.

On this particular morning Earl had been sawing logs, planning to work until around noon. However rain began shortly after he arrived and it soon turned into a heavy downpour which prevented him from further working in the forest. He climbed into the bed of the wagon, pulled the tarp over himself, and sat there eating the food that Evie had prepared and packed for him in a syrup bucket. He was thinking that he would need to soon hitch up the horses and get them into a dry barn. Perhaps he would find someone to come out with him when he returned tomorrow, to help him make some kind of shelter for the horses.

He was quite lost in thought when suddenly he saw a bit of color showing through the trees. Someone wearing blue overalls and a dirty dark brown shirt was walking out of the woods. His hair was long, dark and curling over his shirt collar. On his head was a beaten up old gray hat and he carried a heavy coat over his arm as he stumbled out over the wet stumps of newly cut trees.

The young man saw Earl's wagon, stood very still, and then began to run toward the road.

Earl raised the corner of the tarp and called out, "Just a minute! Were you planning to walk to town? I'm going your way if you want a ride."

The young man stopped, but seemed poised to run again until Earl added, "Here, give me a hand with the horses and we'll soon be on our way."

Earl climbed down from the wagon and went to untie one of his horses from the sycamore tree. The boy stood there a few seconds, uncertain, then walked over and untied the second horse and brought it to the wagon. Earl hitched them up and motioned for the stranger to climb up on the seat.

"My name's Earl Brown," he said offering his hand. The boy shook Earl's hand shyly but said nothing. Earl noticed him glancing back longingly at a basket of apples in the back of the wagon.

"Hungry? Help yourself. There's a bucket back there with a cold biscuit and a piece of fried chicken inside, too, if you want them."

Earl started the horses toward home, through the now gently falling rain. "Where can I drop you in town?"

The boy was chewing chicken and couldn't answer at first. Then he said, "I don't have any place in particular to go."

"Are you just traveling through then?" asked Earl.

"I guess you could say that. I'm on my way out of the mountains."

"Well, I can see you're old enough to be leaving home."

"I'm 18 and I'm leaving to make my own way. Do you live in the next town?"

"Yes, in Norma. You didn't say your name - or is there a reason you don't want to?"

"I'm not wanted, if that's what you mean. You can call me Charlie."

"Well, Charlie, I'm glad to meet you. I have a little furniture shop in town. I live there next door to it. Would you like to have supper at my house? "

"You don't know me! How can you ask a question like that?'

"We're friendly here in Scott County and you look like you could use a meal. I have a wife and daughter. I suppose it's safe to have you eat with us?"

"Of course! I'm just not used to people offering a hand to a perfect stranger."

"I take it you were sleeping in my woods back there?" asked Earl.

"Yes, until the rain woke me. I thought I'd better get a move on, and find a town and hunt for a job. Staying in the woods won't put food in my mouth or a roof over my head."

The sun came out and dried Earl's damp clothes but Charlie still looked soaked to the skin. When they arrived in town, Earl saw Will Wilson's son George coming out of the shop as he talked to a customer.

George saw Earl's team come in and came right over.

"Did you take any orders, George?" Earl asked.

"Yes. And a good one, too. Mr. Morris just ordered a maple bed."

"Good! George this is my friend, Charlie. Will you take care of the team, and show him where the washstand is, please? Make him comfortable until I come back."

George talked to Charlie while he rubbed down and fed the horses. "Earl's a nice man. He's letting me work in his shop so I can make some money for school. That's his wife Evie on the porch next door. She's nice, too."

Earl came into the barn and said, "Come on, you two. Let's go eat."

George excused himself, explaining that he was expected at home. His father was sitting on his porch when he rode up to the house.

"How is everything, Papa? Do you want anything done before I take Winsome to the barn?"

"No, Son. Go ahead."

At supper George told his parents about Charlie. "He came down from the mountain to look for work. Earl invited him to dinner and I expect he will hire him to work at the land he's clearing. He sure needs someone out there right now. For some reason, Earl trusts him."

"I'm glad. He could definitely use some extra hands at the moment," said Will.

Over the next few days Earl and Charlie worked together and became close friends. Charlie told Earl his name was Charlie Tarwater and his family lived up on the west side of Brimstone. His father, Buck, had a moonshine still and forced his three sons to work there.

"That's illegal," commented Earl. "I'm surprised he wants his sons doing it."

"There's money in it; it's easier than farming," Charlie explained. "I didn't want to do it any more, but Pa is a hard man to deal with. We got into an argument and I ran away. He cares for nothing except the money, and he barely gives Mama enough to run the house."

"I expect he wasn't happy that you left."

"No, he needs me. He'll try to find me. I don't want you to have any trouble with him."

Earl said, "I carry a gun. There are always snakes to kill, and when working out in the woods alone, it isn't safe to go unarmed. You should have one too."

Charlie answered, "I had a gun at home. We had to carry one for hunting. I can shoot real good."

"Then I'll buy you one for protection."

Charlie had asked to sleep in the barn, but after a few days he accepted Evie's invitation to sleep in the spare room at their house.

Earl had to spend some time in the shop to take care of the order for the maple bed, so Charlie helped with both the shop and the land clearing.

Charlie occasionally went hunting with Earl's dog Snapper, cooking over an open fire on the property. He put a little shelter over the small spring that was there so they could keep things cold.

The spring air stirred through the trees, the redbuds bloomed and the dogwoods budded. The light greens of the elm and the maples were making the new property a beautiful place. The spruce and pine added their rich dark hues, and the contrast was lovely.

Charlie felt at peace here. He liked Earl and his family. He wished his mother was as happy as Evie.

Earl allowed Charlie to drive the wagon to the new property, and said he would ride out later that day after Mr. Morris came for the new bed. Charlie was busy piling up brush and trimming the logs that would be used to build the cabin. The dog ran around chasing rabbits, while Charlie worked steadily through the morning.

He stopped to eat at noon, then took Snapper into the woods and shot a couple of rabbits which he brought back to camp. He hung a pot over the fire, and while the rabbit stew was cooking, continued to trim limbs off the oak logs, stacking them in a pile to dry so they could be used for fuel.

In the afternoon Earl rode in on his mare.

Charlie said, "I took a break and went hunting this morning. Snapper's a good hunting dog, Earl."

"I'm glad to hear it. What did you find?"

"Two rabbits. They're cooking in the pot right now."

Earl handed Charlie a bucket filled with food from Evie's table.

"I brought a jug of buttermilk, too. Have some."

"Thanks. This will really hit the spot!"

The two men sat on a nearby log while they ate. Charlie wiped his hands on his pants, asking, "aren't you afraid to leave these logs here overnight? They could be dragged right off to the mill."

"You're right. I'm not going to leave them. I plan to camp out here tonight. Do you want to stay with me?"

"Sure, that would be fun," answered Charlie.

"We'll sleep in the wagon and get an early start in the morning."

"I like the outdoors. My brothers and I camped out lots of times," replied Charlie.

They went to work and chopped down two more oaks and stripped the limbs. Then Earl loosed the horses on long ropes so they could graze.

They finished the stewed rabbit, ate cold biscuits, and drank the buttermilk.

"I think we've earned a rest," said Earl.

They leaned back and gazed at the woods.

"Andrew Harness is closing the general store tomorrow and he and his nephew, Luke, are coming to help us raise the logs for the cabin. They'll bring chains so we can pull them into a square and start on the house. Then we can stay out here for several days and build onto it."

He heated some coffee on the campfire, poured them each a cup, and then turned to his new friend.

"I'm glad you came to me, Charlie. I can trust you."

They made their beds in the wagon. The horses stomped for a few minutes, but Earl spoke to them gently, and they soon settled down. The owls called from the trees and crickets began their serenade. Frogs croaked in the creek beds, and soon the two friends were lulled to sleep with dreams of the big work day tomorrow.

At daybreak, Earl woke first to the sounds of birds cheeping in the tree limbs. Charlie stirred when Earl got up.

"It's going to be a beautiful day." Earl took the pail to the spring for fresh water and washed his face. The water was very cold and refreshing. Charlie had a fire started and the coffee pot on when he returned. They used a three legged support over the fire for the pot. Earl got out a frying pan and put in some bacon. They also ate leftover biscuits and a few apples.

"Where will we start today, Earl?" asked Charlie, chewing on a bite of bacon.

"By the time we tend to the horses, Andrew and Luke should be coming along. We need to put up some string to mark the place for the house, first."

Charlie cleared the breakfast things while Earl fed the horses and moved them to a convenient spot to graze. Soon their neighbors drove in. The men helped saw logs to fit, and moved them easily using their heavy chains. About noon the sun was high and they stopped to eat ham that Andrew had brought, and to drink the refreshing water from the spring.

"You have a pretty place here, Earl," said Andrew.

While they were resting, Paul Redmond rode up and reined his horse in with the others.

"I thought you might could use a hand," he said coming to the campsite.

"Glad to see you, Paul." Earl beamed. "How is Kathy? Lydia told Evie just the other day that Stella sure has been missing her since you two married."

"She's just fine, thanks. I'm sure she misses Stella, too."

"Paul, meet Charlie. He's helping me today. Charlie, this is Paul Redmond. He worked for me until Stella's sister won his heart and took him away."

Charlie stuck out his hand and said, "Glad to meet you, Mr. Redmond,"

"I'm just Paul," he said, returning the handshake with a firm grip. Turning to Earl, he added, "It looks like you've been pretty busy. It sure is a nice place you have out here."

With another strong helper, the logs were soon notched and put into place and the cabin took on a look which pleased Earl. He said, "Tomorrow we'll chink the logs. I'll go get some clay from the creek bank. But let's stop now and heat up that coffee pot!"

"You know, you'll soon be ready for the roof to go on and the door to be fixed in place. We could have a party if you like on Saturday and bring the wives," Andrew offered.

"My thoughts exactly," said Earl. "If it doesn't rain."

They feasted on the food that Paul had brought, and rested around the fire, trading stories about other barns and houses they had helped raise over the years, until Andrew finally said, "I better get home."

The three helpers said their goodbyes and started for home.

Charlie replaced the coffee pot with a pot of water to heat for a wash later on and said, "You're lucky, Earl. My folks would never lend a hand to help a neighbor."

"I'm sorry, Charlie, We don't get to choose our parents. I'm glad you got to see how mountain people help their friends. We help each other. It just makes sense. One man can't put a roof on his house alone. The way we do it, everyone can prosper." He brushed his hands together and said, "Let's go gather some wood for tomorrow's breakfast fire and then go hunting!"

"Really?

"Yes. I'm not expecting Andrew to return tomorrow. We'll need something for breakfast besides apples." He called back over his shoulder, "Bring my gun and the game bag from the wagon, while I take care of the horses."

They bathed in the mountain stream and put on fresh clothes when they returned to camp. They dressed the two rabbits and a squirrel they had shot, and put them in the springhouse that Charlie had built.

"Let's try to sleep. If you can't sleep just be quiet and don't wake me."

"Oh, I'll sleep," said Charlie. "I've worked harder today than I have in months! We certainly got a lot done out here the last few days."

"This will be fine for a start," said Earl. "But I need to begin work on the shop soon." He pointed to the spot where he wanted it to be built.

"Evie and I can manage with this cabin, with a lean-to for you for now, but we'll definitely need a larger house by winter."

Silas Wood

Lydia and Martha were busy in the kitchen and Stella was making beds, when she saw, through the window, that a horse and rider were coming up the lane toward her house. She called to the others. The three women drew close together as they watched a tall man get down and approach the porch.

"Quickly, Martha, go and ring the dinner bell," said Lydia. "You stay with me, Stella."

As the man drew nearer, he removed his hat respectfully, revealing sandy red hair and a kind face.

"Excuse me, Ma'am. I'm here to see Mr. Wilson. My name is Silas Wood, and I'm from Brimstone Mountain. Doc McDonald said I should come out and talk to him about a job."

Relieved, Lydia replied, "Have a seat, Mr. Wood," gesturing toward the wooden chair on the porch. "My husband will be here soon."

Will walked up to the back door, asking why the women had rung the bell.

Martha explained, "There's a man here wanting to speak to you. He says he's looking for work."

"Well, I certainly do need an extra hand now that Dent, Kirby and Paul have all gone," Will said. "I'll be glad to talk with him."

Silas Wood was tall and strong, and Will hired him immediately. He found the man could work for hours with no breaks. The two worked well together.

As they rested on the porch one night, Silas told Will and Lydia of his life on the mountain.

"I just didn't want to stay there after my wife died. I sold my little piece of ground and cabin and all I had and came down to Norma."

"I'm real glad you did, Silas. You couldn't have come at a better time. I just wish you would start sleeping here in the house though, instead of the barn. Surely you know us well enough now to sleep in one of our bedrooms."

"Well, maybe I will soon. Right now I like it out there. It's peaceful."

For months the farm flourished. Silas had moved at last into one of the bedrooms, and was quite content.

One day after supper, Silas spoke. "I was wondering, Will, if you would consider selling me a little piece of your property. There's a nice spring just west of your barn, and I could build a simple shelter there. I could have it livable by the winter."

"I'm sure that could be arranged. Mark it off and we'll talk about it."

It was all settled quickly. Silas worked on his land every spare minute and Will was generous to allow him time to do so. He used the boards left over from the shack that Paul and Kirby had made when they first came to work for the Wilsons. The structure had been destroyed by strong winds earlier but the boards were still good. He ordered windows from Andrew's store for the front room.

Silas was proud of himself. He had never been happier.

Martha Wilson

Martha was fretting. She wanted to leave Norma, like her brother had done, and get a job in a town. She had always been close to Dent and missed him so much. She wanted to be off the farm, too. Also, her clothes were wearing out and she yearned for new dresses and stockings. "I have to do so much more around the place than Caroline does. She's spoiled. It isn't fair," she mumbled to herself.

Dent had written that he was going to move with the Chapmans from New River to the town of Kingsport. He explained that Mr. Chapman's brother had asked them to come and open a furniture store with him. Business was better there, he had been told.

Soon the letter came from Kingsport announcing that Dent had married Mr. Chapman's daughter, Delores. They had bought a neat little cottage and were very content. The furniture business was thriving and Dent said he was very satisfied.

This news made Martha even more determined to leave. She wrote to Dent and Delores and asked if she could stay with them for a while. She wrote to Kirby Lee's girl friend Molly, too, for advice on clothing and hair styles in Kingsport. Because she knew her mother would not be in favor of her leaving, she hid the letters she had received in reply.

Martha rode out to visit her friend Kathy after church one Sunday. Once the dishes were done, they went outside to sit on the porch.

Martha went straight to the point. "I want to leave home. I've decided to move to the city, and have a different life, like Dent. I've written to him, and he and Delores wrote back that they would be happy to have me come to their house for a while."

Kathy leaned forward eagerly. "What a wonderful plan."

"But," Martha continued, "I need your help. Would it be possible for me to work for you around your house? I'll be needing some extra money to buy material for new dresses and petticoats."

"Of course," answered Kathy. "What a good idea." Then she sat back in her chair. "But will your parents let you go?"

"I have already talked to Papa about leaving. But I'm expecting Mama to raise a fuss."

"I guess she will. You will certainly be missed over there."

Martha nodded, then added, "And will you help me cut my hair? I'll need a new style if I am going to the city."

At last, when Martha had all her plans in order, she showed the letters to her mother.

"Well, you certainly have been busy, haven't you?" Lydia remarked.

"Yes, Mama, I am determined to go. I'm sure I can find work in Kingsport. The jobs that are available here do not pay enough to live on."

"And what am I supposed to do without you here? Everything will be up to me!"

"Well, you certainly could get more work out of Caroline for one thing. She is lazy and spoiled. It'll do her good to learn to cook and iron and all the chores that I've been doing around here."

Will came in and Martha rushed to him, sure he would take her side.

"Look at my letters, Papa! Dent wants me to come to his house and visit. I do so want to go!"

"I need her here, Will," began Lydia.

"Martha has as much right to go find work as Dent had." Will was gentle but firm with his wife. "She's grown now, Lydia, and needs her chance, too. I'm sure we can manage."

Lydia stalked off to the kitchen.

Will turned to his oldest daughter and said, "Never mind your mother. I'll talk to her. I'll find someone to come in to help out. We'll be fine."

Kathy was elated at the news that her friend was going to have such a good opportunity At once she began helping Martha sew pretty new things for the city, and Martha helped Kathy around her house. Both young women wrote long letters to Dent and Molly.

Finally Martha was ready to go, and was thrilled when her father said, "I'll take you to Kingsport tomorrow. Be ready to go early in the morning."

Martha felt all grown up in her new dress, hat and boots when she walked into the inn with Will two days later. They found Dent waiting for them in the large dining room.

He spotted his sister and ran to hug her. "It's so good to see you both. How was the trip?"

"Just fine," Will answered. "We stopped overnight at a little rooming house and left there early this morning. By the way, I have letters for you."

"I'm always glad to get news from home, Papa. And I can't wait to tell you - I have good news of my own – Delores is pregnant!"

"I'm so glad to hear it, son."

Martha hugged her brother. "How wonderful, Dent! And I can help out while I'm with you two. How's she doing?"

"She's feeling great, and looking good. She's looking forward to your visit."

The three enjoyed a delicious meal and then after visiting for a while, Dent said, "Martha, you and I had best be going. Papa, please come on home with us and spend the night at our house."

"No, Son, it's best that I turn back and begin my journey home as soon as possible. I'll sleep here so I can get up and start early in the morning."

Jasmine and Isobel

One day Dr. McDonald arrived at the Wilson farm and asked to speak to Silas. They all sat on the porch and Lydia brought them cool water to drink.

"Silas, I have just been to Brimstone to your brother Wilbur's house. I was called there after he was involved in a logging accident. He was hurt badly and asked if I could get word to you. He wants you to come as quickly as you can."

"I must go at once," said Silas, "if that's all right with you, Will."

"Yes, of course, go as soon as you can."

A few days later, Silas returned. Will was very glad to see him, but he noticed that he was thinner and little haggard in the face.

"I lost Wilbur," said Silas. "He didn't make it. He was too bad injured."

"I'm so sorry, to hear that, my friend. You need to sleep now. Rest all day tomorrow."

"My brother's family cannot stay there, Will. His widow, Jasmine, and her daughter Isobel are living in a rented house owned by the logging company Wilbur worked for. Now that he is gone, they have to leave. I'm thinking that if I finish my little house soon, I could bring them here."

"That's a good idea. How long have they got to stay in the house?"

"Until the end of the month, she told me." He got up slowly. "I'll just have supper and then go on to bed."

Silas worked hard in the fields to catch up, then on Saturday he worked on his cabin. He sent a letter to his sister-in-law on Brimstone Mountain to tell her to pack up their things. One sunny morning he left with a wagon and two horses on his way to fetch his brother's small family and bring them back to Norma.

Will and Lydia sat on the porch and had a second cup of coffee while they watched Silas driving away.

"I feel so sorry for Silas," said Lydia. "He's a good man."

"Yes, he's a fine person," agreed Will.

"We need to help all we can," said Lydia. "You know his cabin isn't near ready to move into, Will."

"You're right. I was just thinking I ought to go get the windows, if they've arrived, and get Paul to help me put them in. We can fix up some way for them to cook, too."

"There won't be time. Let's have them stay here until his place is more livable."

That evening Will returned from Andrew's store with the windows. "Andrew said he and Paul can come out tomorrow and help me put them in."

"Good. I can get the ladies to come and help, too. It'll be so nice to have a surprise for Silas when he comes back."

"Then I better go milk and get some work done." said Will.

"Stella has already done that, and fed the animals, too. Just come and have some supper and rest."

The next morning Andrew came out to the farm early, leaving Luke in charge of his uncle's general store.

Paul arrived also with his wife, and they brought pots and pans, curtain material, blankets and homespun sheets. "We didn't know if they had any housekeeping things or not," said Kathy.

It was a busy day as all worked steadily putting finishing touches on the little cabin.

"They can make do with this until they have more time," said Lydia, with satisfaction.

Late in the afternoon, the neighbors saw Silas driving the team down the lane. Jasmine and her lovely daughter, whose whole world had been turned upside down, sat beside him. Both she and Isobel missed Wilbur so much and were grieving terribly. To have to leave their home had been almost more than either of them could bear. They were surprised and touched by the warm welcome they received from the Wilsons and all of Silas' neighbors.

Jasmine couldn't believe that everyone was so welcoming and kind; she immediately felt so much better. "What ever would we have done without you, Silas?" She touched his arm with tears in her eyes and hugged Isobel closer.

Lydia and Will welcomed the Wood family and insisted they rest and eat before going to see Silas' cabin. They all sat around the table and Jasmine and Isobel had a chance to get to know their new neighbors.

"George and John can take the wagon to your cabin and unload while you eat," said Will. "George, take care of the horses when you're finished."

Lydia held out her hands to Jasmine, and said, "You're all staying here tonight. You need the rest, and we'll help you tomorrow."

The next morning, Will and Lydia took Silas and his brother's family to the cabin. Silas was amazed to see curtains at the newly installed windows, blankets and sheets, a small table in the lean-to, and even a few pots and pans there.

"All of the neighbors helped us," explained Will. "Now, where do you want your things placed?"

Jasmine and Isobel worked at the cabin the rest of the day while the men went back to the fields.

Will soon hired Jasmine to work in the house with Lydia, who had been sorely missing Martha's help, and the two women became great friends.

Jasmine's daughter was old enough to be very useful in improving the cabin, and with her mother away part of every day she had a chance to grieve in private. She loved singing and made up songs that helped her deal with the loss of both her father and her home in the mountains.

Jasmine and Silas became very close and she depended on him heavily in her need to recover from the loss of her husband. At last, Silas looked into her eyes and said, "We need to think of getting married. People will start gossiping if you and Isobel continue to live in my house."

Jasmine beamed. "We can't have the whole town talking about us now, can we? I would be happy to be your wife, Silas."

Isobel and Jasmine were welcomed into the little Baptist Church down the lane from the general store. Both the young woman and her mother had beautiful singing voices and were asked to sing in the choir. Occasionally they sang solos for their new friends.

The local school teacher, Timothy Johnson, was very attracted to Isobel. He had never before met any woman as tall as he was. Eventually he got himself invited to the Wilsons for dinner so he could meet her in person. She was not at all shy and was glad to meet such a tall, handsome man. Soon they were riding out together after church services and attending various square dances and cake-walks. When the school closed for the season, he asked Silas and Jasmine if he could take her home to meet his parents. The young couple joyfully rode off on a bright sunny morning with Isobel waving to her mother from the seat of his black buggy.

A letter came soon after that from Isobel saying they had married and she would not be returning to Norma for a while.

"I'm so happy for her," said Jasmine. "She needed to find someone who cares for her after all she's been through the past year."

The Clearing

Saturday dawned bright and promised to be a sunny day at "The Clearing," which had become the official name for Earl's property. The entire community was gathering to help Earl and Evie finish raising their new log house.

Wagons were parked everywhere. Soon there was not room for even one more. Andrew took charge, suggesting that the drivers drop off the families and return to their homes. He explained that he would send one of the men out to pick up every driver and bring them back to The Clearing; and of course to return them to their homes later.

Evie sat with Lydia, Maggie, and Maggie's daughter Lenora. She proudly pointed out to her friends where she planned to plant her garden. "I'm so excited that I will have such a grand space for my vegetables; and I hope to plant flowers, too. I want my place to be pretty."

Stella and Kathy spread cloths over the makeshift tables and set out food, plates, silverware and drinking cups.

It was a social gathering as well as a working time for the men. It was loud, too. People called to each other, and the men laughed and joked as they split shingles, then climbed up the ladder and nailed them on the roof.

Lydia's youngest daughter Nancy and Evie's daughter Amy carried water from the spring, proud to be of help; her youngest son Michael, not to be outdone, took the bucket from the girls and brought it the last few feet and set on the table with a swagger.

"This is the best rhubarb pie," said Lydia to the other women, helping herself to seconds, "and have you tasted Maggie's sweet relish?"

Maggie Creech smiled at the compliment, while discreetly changing her position on the wooden chair they had brought out for her. She had insisted on coming even though her back had been giving her problems lately. She attended every community get-together that she possibly could, and she wasn't about to miss this one, although she did promise Lenora that she would not stay too long.

Maggie and her husband had sold the Wilson family the house and land they now called home, years ago, and had been fast friends with them ever since.

"Go cut me a sweet gum stick to brush my teeth with," said Maggie to her son-in-law. When Frank returned he had several with the ends split and ready to use. He gave them out to the children and told them to brush their teeth, too.

Luke took some of the older children up into the woods to hunt a sassafras tree so they could have some tea. "Take Blackie with you to watch for snakes," said Earl.

Evie suggested, "Let's make a place in the wagon so the little ones can nap." The young mothers placed quilts in a wagon bed, making it a comfortable bed.

Luke returned with the children bearing sassafras roots and some ginseng.

"You have a fortune on your property, Earl. There are black walnuts, grapes, persimmons, and hickory and oak trees. The oaks will produce acorns for hog feed, and there's a deep spring higher up. It's as pretty as a picture up there."

Lenora said, "I'll go make us some tea now, and then Mother will have to go home. Frank can come back later." The tea was strained and sweetened, and cups of it were passed around until the sugar ran out. Then Maggie was helped into Frank's buggy, leaning back against a chair that had been turned over to help rest her back. Lenora packed up her empty pots and put them behind her. Turning to Evie, she said, "You're going to love it out here. We'll come to see you as often as we can."

By the end of the day, the small shelter had turned into a cabin complete with chimney and fireplace and a window plus a strong door. At the edge of the woods there even stood a shed where the horses could shelter out of the wind on cold days.

"It's looking mighty good," said Earl, as pleased as could be.

After all had eaten their fill, the group was happy when old Mr. Weems got out his fiddle. He provided lively music for square dancing until everyone was exhausted.

Finally, the wagons were loaded and everyone said goodbye. After the last wagon trundled off down the lane, Charlie said, "Earl, go on home with your family. I'll sleep out here tonight, in the new cabin. I have the dogs and my gun. I'll be safe."

Charlie watched Earl drive away toward Norma with Evie and Amy, as he settled down contentedly in his section of the new house.

Before the milking was done at the Wilson's farm the next morning, rain spattered on the roof. Will smiled and Lydia, and said, "We need the rain, but I'm sure glad Earl got the roof on his cabin."

Annabel Tarwater

One day Charlie and Earl were working on a cedar chest in the furniture shop, when the door opened and a man came in. Charlie kept working and Earl went to the counter at the front.

"Can I help you, Sir?" he asked.

The man spoke roughly. "Yes, I am looking for my boy." At the sound of the man's voice Charlie stood up and looked around.

"There you are," the man said. "I heard you was here."

"What do you want, Pa?"

"I want you to come home, that's what."

"I am not going back, Pa."

"You ungrateful whelp, running off like that!" said Mr. Tarwater loudly. "Sneaking off like a weasel while I was gone."

"Mr. Tarwater, I must ask you to be civil in my shop," Earl spoke up. "Charlie's old enough to make his own decisions."

"You worry your mother," said Buck Tarwater, ignoring the interruption. "She's sick and she needs you, and you don't care enough to come home."

"Mama's sick?" asked Charlie. "What do you mean, sick?"

"She's got a cough and a fever."

"I'll take a doctor to her, Pa ... but I'm not staying there."

"I can't afford no doctor," said Buck.

"I can pay for the doctor. I'm working now."

"Get a move on then. I'll wait outside." Buck snarled as he stalked out.

"Can Dr. McDonald get up the mountain in one day? It's almost midday already," wondered Earl.

"Just barely. But he will have to ride, though. The trail isn't wide enough for his buggy."

"Saddle your horse then. I'll go over and tell the doctor. You'll be safe with your father?"

"He won't try anything with Dr. McDonald along. I don't know what kind of shape my mother's in, Earl, so I'd like to take some food with me."

"Sure. Run over to the house and tell Evie what you need. I'll be back with the doctor as soon as possible. Charlie, be careful. He seems like a rough man to me."

"I'll be careful, don't worry."

Charlie led the doctor up the rickety steps of the front porch and into the untidy front room of the shabby house perched on the side of the mountain.

Annabel Tarwater lay on the rough bed, with quilts pulled up to her chin. A cup and dishes sat on a small table, and the dingy gray windows were open to the outside air.

"I'm Dr. Philip McDonald, Mrs. Tarwater. How are you feeling?"

"My chest is tight and I'm sometimes too warm and sometimes I feel chilled," she answered. "I'm too weak to do my housework; sorry for the way the house looks."

After a short examination, the doctor said, "You have bronchitis, madam. I'll leave you some powders and you must drink plenty of water. Can you come down to my office in Norma in a few days? Perhaps I can get you started on a tonic."

"She's not going anywhere," growled Buck. "We can take care of her, my sons and me."

Dr. McDonald frowned but held his tongue.

Charlie turned to his younger brothers Ben and Bo, who had been standing quietly in the shadows. "There's some food in my saddle bags, if you two will go out with me to get it for Mama."

Annabel reached out for her son's hand. "You will come back though, Charlie, won't you?"

"Yes, Ma, I'll come back and visit. Take your medicine now." Once they were on the path to the village , the doctor said, "Charlie, your mother needs to get down to Norma where she can be helped. I'm not sure she's eating properly."

"Probably not, Doctor," said Charlie. "They didn't have a lot in the kitchen. I guess you could tell my pa and I don't get along."

"I see. Let's hurry. I don't want to be caught on this mountain after dark."

Earl was relieved to see Charlie. He walked out to the stable with him to feed and rub down his horse. Charlie explained about the visit. "I wish I didn't have to leave her up there. She's sick. But what could I do?"

"Nothing, Charlie. You did all you could. She's not able to travel now, and I doubt she would leave anyway. Come on and eat supper. Evie kept it hot for you."

"I need to pay the doctor tomorrow, Earl. I'll have to have some time to go to the bank."

"That'll be fine; but just eat supper now. Help yourself; I'm going to help put Amy to bed. It's something Evie and I like to do together every night."

"You sure love that little girl, don't you?"

"More than you will ever know, Charlie."

The very next Sunday Evie and Earl spoke with Amos Greene about Annabel Tarwater and the Pastor promised that he would have the church gather a few food baskets and send them up the mountain for Annabel and her younger sons.

The Browns were careful not to mention the still, though. They didn't want to cause any unnecessary trouble for Charlie's family.

George and John Wilson

John Wilson poked his older brother, George, on the shoulder. "You promised you'd tell me why you're saving your money."

George stopped hoeing the beans, and wiped his brow.

"That's true. I'll tell you if you'll keep it a secret. Do you remember the two wheel cart that we saw the teacher riding in? Well, I drew up some plans and I hope to make one for myself. Pa said I could go in to see Earl on Saturday. I want to ask him if I can build it in his shop."

"Wow. That'll be great. Can I go with you? I can keep it quiet."

"Sure you can go. I was going to ask you to, anyway. But just keep this between you and me until I let you know that it's all right to tell."

On Saturday, Earl was in his side yard putting up a swing for Amy when George and John rode in and asked to speak to him. He nodded, his hands full of loops of rope. "I'll be with you in a few minutes."

After Earl had heard George's idea and seen the plans he had drawn up, he commented, "These are very good."

"I've been saving up for the lumber. I was hoping you'd let me build it in your shop."

"It's fine with me, if your father approves."

"I had to ask you first, before I could mention it to him," said George. "But I'm pretty sure he will. It would be useful on the farm."

Evie came out and asked the boys to supper.

George politely declined. "No, but thanks. We have to get back."

That very evening, George shared his idea with his father.

Will nodded. "That seems like a very good idea, Son. And it was smart of you to ask Mr. Brown to use his shop."

The next day, the boys asked, "Papa, can we go fishing?"

Will was about to say no, but Silas spoke up, "Let them go, Will. They've worked hard this week, and that is a very clever plan about the cart."

Will agreed, smiling.

So off they went, and Silas said, "Will, your sons are growing up into fine young men."

The Big Storm

Lydia woke up in the night. Lightning lit up the room, and there were deafening claps of thunder. She got up and put on her wrapper. She was reminded of the terrible storm that had taken her good friend, Flora Lawson, Kathy and Stella's mother, and destroyed their house. Even though it had been several years ago, it still burned in her memory.

Will got up too and sat in the kitchen with her. "Do you want me to build a fire, Lydia?"

"No, thank you, though. I just want to wait out this storm. It's a bad one."

Will agreed, and after a very loud crash said, "I expect I'll have a big mess to clean up after that hail hits the corn stalks and bean plants."

"I worry about Kathy on nights like this. Ever since she lost her mother, she has a hard time with bad weather, specially with lightning."

George joined them at the table, still pulling his trousers on over his night shirt. Rain beat hard on the roof, wind rattled the windows, and gusts blew down the chimney. Hail pounded on the porch.

John came in buttoning up his shirt, and just as he pulled out a chair to sit down with the others, they were all startled by a brilliant flash and simultaneous deafening crack of thunder. Will jumped up to look out the windows to the east.

"It's the barn!" he shouted. "It's hit the barn! Quick, boys. Get your boots on. Lydia, get wet towels. We have to get the stock out!"

They were at the barn quickly. Silas and Jasmine came running from their place. The horses were screaming hysterically in terror as flames leaped from the loft and spilled down the walls.

Will threw blankets over the horses' heads and pulled them outside. George and John with wet towels over their faces led the two Jersey cows out behind Will. The flames ate through the barn boards furiously, as the rain pelted down. Silas grabbed the blankets they had used for the horses and threw them over the buggy, while Jasmine, George and John pushed from behind. They finally managed to get it rolled out the barn door to safety.

The entire roof collapsed in a fiery pile. Will checked his family; all were out except John. He was still inside, blinded by the smoke. Will and George rushed back in, grabbed him by the shirt, and guided him out to the barnyard. His hair was on fire. Will threw him to the ground and smothered the flames with the blankets.

Jasmine screamed suddenly and ran down the lane. Silas said, "Go after her, George, she's in shock. We'll see to John." He picked John up gently and carried him toward his own house, which was closer than the Wilson's.

The barn continued to burn fiercely until it was finally quenched by the rain. The farm animals had run into the woods, and Will and Lydia followed behind Silas onto the porch of his cabin. The blackness disappeared when Lydia lit a lamp in the front room and set it on the mantel, flooding the place with light. Will stripped the shirt from his son's body to assess the wounds. John's hair was burned to the scalp, and his face was blackened. He choked and sputtered when he tried to talk. The collar of his shirt was gone, and angry looking red blisters were rising on his skin.

"We need the doctor, Silas," said Will.

"I'll saddle up right away."

Lydia knelt beside John trying to comfort him through her own tears.

Will pulled her away gently. "Lydia, go home and get into dry clothes and see about the children and Jasmine." He knew he had to get her away from John before she became hysterical.

Lydia ran toward the house guided by the light in her own windows. George was there holding Jasmine, who was sobbing quietly. "I've got her calmed down now, Mama. How's John?"

"He's burned pretty bad. Silas has gone for the doctor." She was shaking, not realizing she was in shock, also. She checked on the younger children, and was reassured when she saw Nancy and Michael sleeping peacefully, unaware of all that was going on around them.

"I've got to go back and check on John," she said, shaking.

"Mama, listen to me. You're in shock, too. Go change clothes; take Jasmine with you. You both need to change into something dry."

The two women brought clothes from the bedroom and dressed by the fire that George had stoked. Lydia put on coffee, all the while talking softly to Jasmine, calming herself without realizing it. "Silas will be back with Dr. McDonald soon. I want you to stay here with the children. Go to bed if you want to. I'll go back so I can be there if Will needs me."

Lydia heard a commotion outside. The neighbors were coming. Paul and Earl ran from their wagons as Lydia threw open the door. She didn't want the knocking to wake the children.

"We saw the smoke, Lydia. What's happened?"

"It's the barn. It's gone. John's been injured. He and Will are at Silas' cabin. Go on over there. I have to stay and get Jasmine tucked in."

Frank Jeffers, Maggie Creech's son-in-law, pulled in just then, and Earl came over and explained what had happened. Dr. McDonald drove in also and went straight to Silas' cabin. Earl sent Silas to see about Jasmine, then led the doctor to John.

"Bring more light," said the doctor, "Let me see how bad this is."

Will held a lantern closer to John, who lay on the bed in one of Silas' nightshirts.

The doctor examined him, then declared, "He's lucky. It could have been a lot worse. He'll be all right in time." He gave John a sedative, and dressed his burns. Is anyone else hurt?"

Will showed him a burn on his arm.

"I'll clean that up, too, when I come back. I need to make sure Jasmine gets a sedative and gets some rest."

At the Wilson home, the doctor talked to Jasmine and gave her some powders mixed in water. "Sleep late tomorrow," he said. "Lydia, don't worry. John has some burns on his neck and scalp. It will take a while, but it will heal and his hair will grow back. Right now everybody needs to get some rest."

He returned to Silas' cabin, cleaned Will's arm, and put some salve on the wound. "I need to go. I have patients in the morning; but I'll come back out here when I've finished."

Will didn't want to see the damage to his fields. He just wanted to sleep for hours. He joined Lydia on a pile of quilts on the floor, and fell deeply asleep.

Daylight came soon after. The sun burned off the fog, and dried what remained of the barn.

Jasmine awoke feeling much better. She cared for the children, making sure the little ones got a good breakfast, and keeping them quiet. At Silas', John slept deeply until the third day, when he awoke and asked for water. Lydia got him to eat some soup as well; then he lay on his side gazing out the front door of the cabin.

The men went out and found the livestock in the nearby fields, and cared for them. They rode over the farm to assess the damage of hail to the crops, finding that the corn had straightened up. Will looked over the alfalfa and the rows of corn. "It looks pretty good, considering. The tomatoes will recover in time, and the blackberries are ready to pick now. We've got plenty of work ahead of us, Silas."

"It'll be good for you to get into it and get your mind off all that has happened."

The neighbors gathered the fruit that had been knocked from the trees and took it home to be prepared for cooking. The wives soon had delicious pies in their ovens, much to everyone's delight.

****

As soon as George heard that Dr. McDonald had said it would be all right for John to return home by the end of the week, he began planning a surprise for his brother. On Tuesday he asked Will for permission to go into town, promising to return soon.

Will readily agreed. "I want you to deliver some honey to the inn, anyway. Tell the innkeeper I'll bring in the rest of the order soon. Put the money into my account at the bank."

George did his chores quickly, and after delivering the honey and stopping by the bank, he went straight to the furniture shop.

On Saturday the doctor arrived at the Woods' just as Jasmine was cooking breakfast. He checked John's bandages and declared him well enough to go home, then sat down at the table.

"Just a few minutes, Jasmine. I'd like a cup of coffee before I get started this morning." The doctor kept watching from the porch down the lane toward the Wilson house.

"What is it, Doc? Do you see Papa coming yet?" John was eager to get started for home.

"Not yet." He sipped his coffee and asked Jasmine for a buttered biscuit. He munched happily.

Finally he rose and walked off the porch, "I see someone coming. It won't be long now." He helped John up so he could sit on the porch in a rocker.

It wasn't Will who drove into the yard after all. John was thrilled to see that it was George who was driving his horse, Winsome, pulling a beautiful two wheeled cart made of oak.

"How do you like my cart, John?" he called, "I've come to take you home in style."

The doctor and George helped John down off the porch. George was smiling broadly at his brother.

"So that's why Doc was stalling," John grinned. "That's great, George. Help me in. I can't wait another minute."

Jasmine stood laughing as she watched the cart roll down the lane with the doctor's buggy following behind.

At the Wilson house everyone was there to welcome the patient home.

Lydia invited the doctor to come in for coffee, but he explained that he had already loitered around enough for one morning. "I'll come back in a few days, though, to see how he's doing."

Will's New Barn

Andrew helped Stella into the buggy, with the huge basket of fried chicken she had prepared, and they started out for the Wilson house. On the way, they caught up with Earl and Evie who were bringing little Amy and Maggie Creech. In the back of their buggy there was a pot of stewed ham with onions and potatoes. Amy carried a basket of corn meal muffins on her lap. Maggie held a pie, and Evie had a jar of pickled beets. Already there were other wagons at the house and the porch and yard were full of neighbors. Men were crowded in the area where the new barn was to go up.

They saw logs piled there, and a pair of barn doors on the ground with many pieces of lumber and various tools.

Will shook hands with Andrew and hugged all the ladies including little Amy, making her feel just like a grown up lady.

"Lydia's inside, Maggie. Go on in. Come with me, Andy. We're getting the logs ready now."

Stella rushed to see her father, Sam Lawson, who was sitting under an elm tree talking with her sister Kathy and her husband Paul. Two chairs sat nearby and soon George and John came and sat in them, chatting and waving to the newcomers.

Sam commented, "I see your hair is coming in, John."

"Yes, it is. And the doctor says I need to leave my neck open to the air so it can heal faster. I'm doing real good. Glad you could come."

Many of the neighbors stopped by to ask John how he was doing, and he was proud to tell them all that the new skin was growing, and that he felt great.

The men gathered and began to arrange the logs, while the ladies covered the makeshift tables with cloths and set the food there, while Lydia and Jasmine were still inside, cooking. More wagons came in and the men took the horses to the pasture and set water for them. More food appeared. Soon there was no more room, and the additional dishes had to be taken inside. Silverware and drinking cups were placed on the tables. The children played tag and other games and laughed gaily. It was a happy time for them, as well as the adults. The caulk was ready and the men built the walls higher and higher. Some of the children joined George in filling in the cracks with caulking.

When the sun was overhead they all stopped to rest. The ladies brought out jugs of buttermilk and tea, and told the folks to go to the tables and fill their plates.

It was an enormous feast. Maggie helped serve until her friends saw she was tired and persuaded her to sit in a rocker and eat her dinner, where she could visit with Lenora and Frank and all the neighbors.

The men returned to the barn and soon the roof was ready to go on. All the men helped set up ladders, bring more lumber, and nail shingles on the roof.

John finally grew tired and went inside to rest. At last, Maggie said she wanted to lie down a while, also. The younger ladies cleaned up the yard and removed the plates and silverware, put cloths over the remaining food, and went to sit under the trees to visit with each other.

Lydia heard a shout from down the lane, and was first to see her eldest son driving toward them. Dent Wilson helped his wife, Delores, with their little son, Lonnie, down from their buggy. After seeing to the horses, he went to see his mother and George and was told that John was inside resting. "I want to go and talk to John, if he isn't asleep. I'll be quiet and not wake the babies. I will eat, Mama, don't worry about that!"

Lydia said, "Go on in. He'll be so happy to see you, son."

Lydia hugged her daughter-in-law and was thrilled when her little grandson climbed up in her lap and let her cover him with kisses.

Evie came over and said, "Come on, Lonnie, you and I will go see what you want to eat." She scooped up the little boy and headed for the tables, while Delores followed with Lydia at a more leisurely pace.

John came awake as Dent touched his hand and the two cried in each other's arms.

"I didn't know you were coming, brother," said John.

"We just got here," said Dent. "How are you feeling? "

"I'm doing good," said John. "It's been pretty rough, I can tell you. We hated to lose the barn, and Papa's arm was burned, but it's all healed now. Look at my new hair. Isn't it awful?"

Dent agreed, laughing at its scraggly appearance, then said, "there's no more time for you to rest. Come and meet my wife and son!"

Dent introduced Deloris and Lonny to everyone, then loaded plates for himself and Deloris and found them a place to sit near Will and Lydia. John got another piece of pie and some cider and sat with them, too.

Lonnie took a turn sitting on his grandfather's knee. Will fondly allowed him to pat his face and pull at his hair.

"Martha sends her love," said Dent. "I have letters for you both."

Lydia sat reading the letters, wiping a tear every now and then, looking up to gaze at her family.

When Dent had finished eating a big piece of cherry pie, he said, "I'll come and help, Papa. I'm not tired at all." He climbed a ladder, grabbed a hammer, and began nailing shingles in place; he was happy to be with his family and friends.

Frank and Sam finished the barn doors. Another neighbor put the frame in place and nailed it securely. Some of the children handed nails to the workers. Everyone wanted to be a part of the barn raising and to help get it built and ready for Will and Lydia.

After it was declared finished except for the inside stalls and tack room, there was more eating. Mr. Weems got out his fiddle from his wagon and the dancing started. Silas and Jasmine took turns playing the guitar, and Jasmine sung a few songs on request.

Pastor Greene and his wife arrived and Dr. McDonald and his wife, also. Lydia invited them to eat, assuring them there was plenty more food inside the house.

Dr. McDonald checked John's neck. "Let me just bandage this up first. We don't want it to get infected. I think he's had enough air for today."

When Mr. Weems started fiddling a merry tune, Will grabbed Lydia's hand and insisted she dance a jig with him. Dent did the same with Delores.

Pastor Greene smiled as he watched the scene, and asked God to bless them all.

Earl and Evie Brown's New Cabin

Things were busy at The Clearing. Earl was determined to get his new cabin ready before cold weather. He and Charlie both spent long days working at the shop in town, then went out almost every evening to finish the shop on the new property. The structure was already snug, with two rooms and a loft for Charlie's bed.

Earl brought beds from the house, and a cook stove, too. He built a table and benches and placed a water bench outside the kitchen door. Then he fashioned a small stoop so they could have an entrance in cold weather until he could build a proper porch to suit Evie.

He and Charlie went to the woods and chopped down the trees he had marked, then used the horses with heavy chains to drag them down out of the forest so Charlie could trim off the branches.

The two men often continued working until it grew too dark to see, and then they eagerly sought their blankets.

Stella and Andrew Harness

Andrew Harness was doing very well. His parents had decided to move back up to their property on Brimstone Mountain, and they left their house, the General Store, and the Post Office to him.

He had married Stella Lawson, and together they had done wonders with the house. He added a big porch and rebuilt the kitchen. He included a large room upstairs so his cousin Luke, who helped him in the store, could live with them there.

Stella was delighted with the additional space and immediately made new curtains and chair covers. Andrew ordered a sofa for her from Knoxville that was the envy of her family and neighbors. She planted four-o'clocks in her back yard, and her sister Kathy shared several rose bush cuttings with her, so the house was bright and cheery outside as well as inside.

The young couple were expecting their first baby, and looked forward eagerly to the event.

Stella rested on the sofa after cooking a larger meal than usual; she planned to have leftovers for at least one more meal the next day. Her back ached, and she felt sure her time was near. Her little dog, Tommy, was waiting expectantly at the door.

"Oh, I just can't take you out right now, Tommy. Maybe Luke will be here soon." She pulled herself up to a sitting position, just as Luke knocked on the inner door that led from the store.

"Luke, I'm glad to see you. Will you let Tommy out, and then go tell Andrew that I think it's time to go for the doctor?"

Luke stared a couple of seconds, and then lunged for the door. Tommy scooted out as he opened it. "I'll hurry," he said.

He ran first back to the shop and announced, "Go to Stella, Andy. I'll go for the doctor, and then watch the store for you.

Stella lay back with perspiration on her face, feeling a little frightened. Andrew held her hand while Dr. McDonald checked her pulse.

"Go back to the store, Andrew. I'll have a look. I'll call you if I need you. Come, Stella, let me help you to the bedroom. It really isn't quite your time yet, you know."

Later to doctor said to Andrew, "I think she's having twins."

"Twins?" Andrew sat down in the first chair he could find. "Twins? That's ... that's wonderful!"

"She'll need plenty of rest. Perhaps you should ask one or two of her younger sisters to come help out for a while."

Andrew said, "That's a good idea. I think I'll ask both Malinda and Dora to come. They are each too young to handle it all, but together they should be fine. We have a room they can share now that we have expanded."

Malinda and Dora were happy to come and help out. They cooked, cared for Stella and the house, and did laundry, when they weren't taking classes at the little schoolhouse. Stella lay on the sofa or in her bedroom and waited impatiently for her twins to be born.

Nancy Wilson

Nancy was watching her mother lining a wooden cradle with soft pink fabric. "What're you doing, Mama?" she asked.

Lydia smiled at her. "Would you like to see a little baby come to Silas and Jasmine's house?"

"Oh, yes, Mama. That would be nice."

"Well, that's why I'm fixing this cradle. Jasmine is going to be a mama just like me."

"Did I sleep in this cradle when I was small?" Nancy leaned in to take a closer look.

"Yes, and so did Mike. Now let Mama finish the seams. If you'll fetch the thread for me you can tell Jasmine that you helped make the pillow."

"Do you think I could have a cradle like that for my doll?"

"We'll see. That would be nice, wouldn't it? Maybe you can ask for one for Christmas."

Kathy and Paul Redmond

Paul Redmond could not stop smiling. Kathy had just told him she was pregnant, too.

The timing couldn't be better. He had found full time work at the grist mill, and had finally finished the repairs on the damage that had been done to her family's home in the great storm two years earlier (the one that had also taken her mother's life.)

Kathy no longer had nightmares about the storm. She felt uneasy whenever she saw lightning or heard thunder, but no longer cried with every rumble. She felt strong and ready for the responsibility of a new baby.

Sam and all his daughters still put flowers on Flora's grave regularly, and he still mourned for her, but he was once again able to find pleasure in everyday things and life was going smoothly for him now. He was comfortable with Kathy and Paul living with him, and was ecstatic with the knowledge that his two elder daughters were both going to give him grandchildren soon.

Thanksgiving

It was cold in Norma on Thanksgiving. The Wilsons were happy, with company all over the house. Dent and Delores brought little Lonnie and came for two days. Caroline, their middle daughter, was home from school for a week.

Martha had sent letters of good wishes from Kingsport, reporting that she was doing well working for a dressmaker there who owned her own shop. Although Will and Lydia missed her terribly, they were pleased to hear of her success.

Timothy and Isobel Johnson came by the Wilsons' on their way back to their home in Carey after visiting Silas and Jasmine and their new baby boy, Silas Wilson Woods. They couldn't stop talking about how cute "Little Si" was.

"He's such a happy baby," Isobel raved.

The dinner included fresh turkey and venison as well as all the vegetables and fruit preserves Lydia and her girls had put up last season, plus honey and biscuits and of course several kinds of pies.

After dinner, while everyone was relaxing around the fire, talking and playing games, Caroline decided to walk on over to see the Woods' baby for herself. Isobel had mentioned that it might snow later, and Caroline didn't want to miss seeing him before she had to leave to go back to school in Knoxville.

Little Si was as cute as Isobel had promised. Caroline was enthralled. "He's a real charmer!"

Silas and Jasmine both beamed at the compliment.

Caroline asked to hold the baby on her lap, and she rocked him gently as she caught up on the news from their household.

"I'm going to add on to the house when spring comes," Silas announced proudly. "Your father and I are already drawing plans."

"Will you be buying from the mill or using your own timber?"

"There's plenty to cut right here. I'll make it a log house with my own trees. I'm going to add bee hives, too, to help with expenses. Andrew said he never has enough honey to fill his orders."

Caroline stayed with her friends until darkness fell, then she stood, saying, "oh, I really must go. Papa will be out looking for me. I didn't mean to stay so long."

George Wilson

Earl looked up from sanding a cedar chest at his shop just as George and John Wilson stopped by.

"You're just in time, George; come help me finish sanding this cedar chest."

Excited to share the plans he was making for his future, George started talking as soon as his hands touched the wood.

"I'm saving my money to get my own horse and buggy, Earl. And then I plan to go to school in Kingsport for engineering."

"Well, I think that's a fine idea. But where will you live?"

"I've already thought of that. I've written to Dent and he and Delores have offered to let me live with them for a while, just like they did when Martha set out on her own."

John had already heard his big brother's plans, so he wandered on over next door to see Evie. He wanted to find out what Amy wanted for Christmas; plus he was sure he would find fried pies or maybe some cookies there. As soon as she saw him, Evie asked him to sit down and tell her all the news from the Wilsons; of course, she also handed him a big molasses cookie.

Charlie's Accident

Charlie rode out to check on the cabin at The Clearing for Earl. They had left the two dogs there to guard the place, but as soon as he neared the turnoff, he sensed something was wrong. He didn't see either dog, and they would normally run right out when they heard him coming. He urged his horse forward and jumped down. There was debris all over the yard. Tree limbs, broken bottles, and jars. He saw that the window was broken out, and he looked inside through a gaping hole.

What he saw made him sick. The inside was strewn with dishes, glasses and dirty spoons. A battered coffee pot lay in the ashes on the cold hearth. He went around to the front, and easily opened the door, for the lock had been broken. The bed was torn up with pillows on the floor.

He had little doubt who had been here. He didn't stay to check the supplies. Earl's dog Blackie whimpered and came up to him; he followed him to the edge of the woods where he found the other dog, Snapper, dead, shot through the head.

Charlie mounted and rode off down the road at a gallop toward Norma, rushing to get back to Earl's shop.

A bitter wind had come up, and he quickly became chilled. He hadn't counted on a change in the weather. His light-weight coat was of little comfort. His hat flew off and landed in a fast moving stream that curved down into the woods. Suddenly he saw a wagon racing down the hill with the reins hanging down and no driver. Almost numb with cold and fright, Charlie pulled over to the side of the muddy road, but not in time. The runaway team was on him. His horse reared and threw him onto the cold ground on the other side of the ditch. Stunned, he lay there helplessly as the wagon disappeared down the road in the other direction.

Blackness descended on Charlie there in the field of dead weeds, cold mud and thick brush by the side of the road.

Thelma Dubarry was rushing home in her little buggy. She was late. Her father was home alone with her little boy, and the weather had turned bad. The trees were bending in the biting wind. As she rounded a sharp curve, she saw a touch of color and movement by the side of the road. Thinking it might be an old shawl or other useful fabric, she stopped the horse to look. She was startled to see a man lying there moaning.

"I just can't leave him here if he's badly hurt," she thought. She tied Goldie to a shrub and crossed the ditch. As she grew closer she could see that he had a deep cut on his forehead.

Charlie opened his eyes and saw Thelma as she tried to lift him; he tried to get up but fell back in pain. "She's so dainty," he thought. Then blackness came down again.

When Charlie next opened his eyes, he was in the bed of a moving wagon. Pain shot through his head and arm. He bit his lip to keep from crying out. Someone had stopped and was taking him somewhere. He remembered the young girl; but no, she was too small to have lifted him. It couldn't be her.

He tried to raise his head to see the driver, but the pain was too much, and he fell back, unconscious.

****

Thelma was tired and chilled. She had been outside to get her packages from the buggy. She closed the door behind her and looked over at the man lying on her sofa. He was as pale as a sheet and had blood on his forehead.

She was glad to get out of her cloak and gloves and stir up the fire with another chunk of wood. She got a pan of warm water and a cloth and some salve and went to the injured man. She had just started to clean the dried blood away when her father came in from putting the buggy away. He removed his coat and leaned a pair of crutches against the fireplace. He turned to Thelma. "How is he?"

"Still out," said Thelma. "He's bad hurt, Papa. I can't ride for help now. It would be dark before I got to the doctor's office."

"You're right," said Rube. "We'll just do the best we can for him until morning."

When she applied the cloth again, Charlie groaned and grabbed at her hand.

"Easy," said Thelma. "You're safe. You're all right. Easy, now." Her voice was calm and reassuring.

Charlie said, "Where am I?"

"In my house. I'm Thelma Dubarry and this is my father, Rueben Miller. I found you hurt by the side of the road. There's no way I can ride for help tonight. My father can't go either. He's hurt, too."

"It's my knee," explained Rube. "I'll be okay in a few days."

"I can go for the doctor at first light," said Thelma. "What's your name?"

"Charlie Tarwater. My horse threw me, when a runaway team came by and scared him. I expect he went back home. I hope so." He closed his eyes again.

"Here, let me bandage the cut. Then you should try to drink some water. I'll fix you something to eat as soon as I can."

Reuben said, "Thelma, there's a bit of laudanum left that the doctor sent for me when I hurt my knee. He can have some of that."

"Thanks, Papa. I'll do that."

She carried the pan toward the back of the cabin. Setting it down with one hand, she pulled back the curtain that hid a small bed with the other. She lifted a baby, who had just begun to cry. "Can you hold Matthew while I heat supper, Papa?"

"Sure, hand him to me. Go ahead and start the stew warming; then Charlie can eat before you give him the medicine."

"That's a good idea." She swung the iron pot around on the hob and stirred it with a long handled ladle. When she was satisfied that it was warm enough, she filled a small bowl for Charlie. He managed to eat a few bites, then accepted a spoonful of the laudanum.

Charlie lay all night on the sofa covered by two warm blankets, and slept because of the medicine. He woke with a dry mouth and looked around, remembering where he was. The fire was almost out. He tried to move but pain shot down his arm again so he lay still and soon slept again.

He stirred again later when he heard the sounds of Rueben building a fire in the fireplace.

He saw that Charlie was awake. "Was it a bad night?" he asked.

"I slept fine," said Charlie. "That was good medicine. Thanks. But, can you tell me how I came to be here on your sofa?"

"My daughter found you unconscious by the side of the road in a field."

"But I know she's too small to have lifted me alone ..." Charlie started.

Reuben held up his hand. "Wait. A man who was passing by stopped to help. He got you into his wagon, and they brought you here. He had to leave because he had gotten word that there was an emergency at his home. It was good of him to help. He even took the time to get you inside here before he went on his way."

"Good morning. How are you today?" A cheerful voice met Charlie's ear.

The curtain was pulled back and Thelma emerged carrying a smiling baby.

Charlie felt better at once.

"My head and my arm still hurt but I'm much better," said Charlie. "I'm very grateful for what you did, and I'll be able to pay you in a few days."

"Don't worry about paying us. As soon as we have breakfast, I'll go for the doctor in Norma. Can I find your folks for you? They must be worried."

"Yes, please. I'm staying at the home of Earl Brown. He has a furniture shop right across from the general store. If you'll stop there and tell someone, they'll come for me. I'll be in your debt."

****

Earl came into his house with a deep frown on his forehead.

"What's the matter, Earl?" asked Evie.

He reached for her hand, and led her to sit by the fire.

"Is Amy asleep?"

"Yes. She won't hear you. Tell me what's wrong."

"We don't know where Charlie is. We found his horse riderless on the road and several of us went

83

looking for him. We knew he had gone out earlier to check on the cabin."

"Did you go there?"

"Yes, and that's why I'm so worried. The cabin is a mess. The window is broken and the lock has been shot off the door. One of my dogs was shot and killed. There was no sign of Charlie."

"Oh, Earl," Evie gasped, gripping his hand tightly. "Where could he be?"

"I don't know. I'm worried that his father has done something. Whether Charlie caught him and his buddies there I have no way of knowing. If he's with his father, there's nothing we can do, Evie; he's a grown man."

"I don't believe he went willingly, Earl. He wouldn't leave us like that. He could be hurt somewhere."

"I know, Evie. But let's sleep, now. We'll search more in the morning." Earl lay beside Evie all night, but he didn't sleep much; he was too tense with worry. He hoped that Charlie's father had not mistreated him in some way. He realized he cared for Charlie as if he were kin. The riderless horse was proof enough that something was seriously wrong. He desperately wanted morning to come so he could go searching for Charlie again.

****

Charlie lay on the sofa watching the clock on the mantel. Sweat dampened his brow and the pain began to grow more intense. Thelma would bring Dr. McDonald, and maybe Earl too. It seemed the clock moved awfully slowly.

He could hear Reuben talking softly to the baby as he rocked him gently. Charlie wondered, "Where's the father? Was she married, this girl with dark hair down her back and thick dark eyelashes? Her name was different from her father's. She must be married, but where was he? Maybe her husband was dead?"

****

As soon as Earl ate a biscuit and sausage and swallowed his coffee in the early morning, he rushed out to saddle his horse.

"Don't worry, Evie. I'll find him," he called over his shoulder. "If he hasn't gone back to the mountain, I'll find him." He kissed his wife and Amy, and rode off as fast as his horse would take him.

The sun was barely showing over the mountain, and the clouds were pink and silver in the pale blue sky.

The chill of the morning hit his face as he rode along toward his cleared land. He had begun to pull over to the side to allow a black buggy to pass, when it slowed and a young woman held up her hand and motioned for him to stop.

"I wonder if you might know Earl Brown?"

"Yes, I'm Earl Brown."

"I hoped you would be. I was told you might be out searching this morning for Charlie Tarwater. He's hurt."

"Hurt? How bad, Miss?"

"He may have a broken arm, and he has a gash on his forehead. He's safe now, and resting at my house. I'll go on to get the doctor. You should keep going to

Jamestown road, then take the first right turn and go about a mile. My house is the first log house you'll see. My father's there with Charlie."

"Thank you so much. I'll go right there." Earl started to leave, then tuned back. "Miss, if you don't mind, when you get to Norma will you have someone tell my wife – she's Evie Brown – that Charlie's going to be okay? She's as worried as I've been."

Earl followed her directions and found the cabin. He knocked on the door.

Reuben came and threw it open.

"My name's Earl Brown. I'm looking for Charlie."

"Come on in. He's here." Rube gestured toward the sofa, then hobbled back to the bed where little Matthew had been awakened by the noise.

Earl pulled up a chair next to the sofa. "Charlie," he started. But that was all he could say.

"Did you meet Thelma on the road?" Charlie asked.

"I did. She told me where to find you. Is your arm broken?"

"I think so. It hurts really bad."

He went on to explain all that had happened.

"We found your horse. He's safe at home," said Earl.

"Thanks for taking care of him for me. Oh, will you help Mr. Miller? He can't bring the baby to the fire on those crutches."

"Of course." Earl went back to the curtained area and said, "I'll help you, sir. Just go sit in the rocker and I'll bring the baby to you."

"I'm obliged," said Rube, hobbling over to the rocker.

Dr. McDonald came in with Thelma, set Charlie's arm with splints he had brought, then gave him a glass of brandy. He eased Charlie back on the sofa and said, "It's a clean break, Charlie. That's good. Can you stand? If you can, we'll get you home."

"I'm not sure if I can, but I'll sure try."

After several attempts, Charlie was able to get on his feet.

Earl and the doctor helped him get outside and into the buggy for the ride home. "Thanks again, Mr. Miller, Thelma. We sure appreciate your kindness to our friend." Earl pressed a few bills into Rube's hand.

Later the doctor came to Earl's house, put a more sturdy cast on Charlie's arm, and told Evie and Earl how to take care of him. He left some powders for them to give him for the pain.

Before he slept, they all talked about the damage to The Clearing.

"I'm sure my father did all that, Earl. Just for spite. I'm sorry. I know it isn't my fault, but I feel really bad that he did that."

"We won't worry about that now. Get some sleep. I'm just glad you're safe and will survive the accident."

They took good care of Charlie. Amy was fascinated with the whole situation. She was happy to help, bringing him his meals and water to drink. Since Charlie had one good hand, he drew pictures for her and told her stories. Evie treated him to his favorite foods.

On Saturday, Charlie felt strong enough to ride out to The Clearing with Earl. It was as Charlie had seen it last and he walked through looking at all the devastation.

"We don't know that it was Buck who did this. It could have been some drifters." Earl tried to soothe his friend.

"I guess, but I still think my Pa had something to do with it."

Christmas

Christmas came to the foothills of Brimstone Mountain, and everyone was ready. Santa Claus brought the little ones just what they wanted: a doll cradle for Nancy, just like the one she had had as a baby, and which she immediately loved, and for Michael a wooden dancing man on a string and board, and a wooden wagon.

Will had ordered a new rocking chair from Earl for Lydia. He had made a sled for Michael and Nancy to use in the snow. Other gifts arrived from Martha and Dent.

The house was filled with the aroma of roast turkey and pumpkin pie. Jasmine had made a blackberry jam cake, and Kathy had sent over an apple stack cake, which she knew was a favorite of Will's. Jasmine and Silas led them in Christmas carols with the guitar. Little Si, in his basket, charmed everyone with his smiles. He of course received many presents of clothes from all the girls and women.

Caroline came home, bringing many gifts. Perhaps the most special was a water color she had painted especially for Jasmine and Silas. The touching portrait of her holding her son brought Jasmine to tears; even Silas had to discreetly rub his hand across his eyes.

On Christmas morning the Wilson family joined their neighbors at the little white Baptist Church in Norma for a special Christmas program. Caroline and Jasmine sang a moving version of *Silent Night,* which they had practiced earlier at home. The Pastor, Amos Greene, read the Christmas story, then he and his wife gave out small bags with candy, nuts and an apple to each congregant.

The pastor's son, Eli, who was also visiting for the holidays, took Caroline home from church in his fine carriage.

"Caroline, perhaps I may call on you in Knoxville?" he asked.

"Of course. I would like that very much," she smiled.

After the holidays Will and Silas took Caroline to catch the train at the new spur that had been built to take timber from Norma to Knoxville. She was wearing a new cloak and bonnet, and was fairly loaded down with packets. Lydia had made a new quilt, and Jasmine had made a matching pillow, for her to take back for her room at school.

Caroline was excited to be returning to the city; she always enjoyed her studies - and this time she was also looking forward to seeing Eli again.

Will, however, was sad to see her go. He always felt like something was missing when his beautiful daughter was away from home, even though he was very proud of her accomplishments and knew she had to have her education to support her love of art.

Spring

Spring arrived in the foothills, announcing itself with redbuds, locust and blooming dogwoods. The mountains were alive with color and the April breezes exhilarated Charlie who had his cast removed and was ready to assume all of his duties. Robins, thrushes and blue jays returned with their birdcalls, while mockingbirds built nests in the holly bushes.

While Evie and Amy set to work finishing up the cabin, Earl and Charlie made a bonfire of the rubbish.

The wood smoke was aromatic and they liked smelling it. They were ready to continue improving his property. They wanted to forget the past months.

The two men put new glass in the window, then took their axes and crosscut saws to cut trees farther up in the woods, while Amy and Evie carried water from the spring and started a small campfire to prepare a big pot of soup for their midday meal.

Earl and Charlie talked over the plans for the shop and house after they finished eating the soup, but were still chewing on the bread and fruit that Evie had brought from home.

"I'm going to change the house, and make it bigger than it was originally, Charlie. Look, you can have this space for your own bedroom."

Charlie smiled. "That's mighty kind of you."

They burned out the stumps so they could plant a few rows of vegetables; and then cleared even more so Evie and Amy could have a place for roses.

Evie used a hoe to dig up some ground by the cabin wall to plant flowers. Amy was not at all afraid of the fat earthworms that they found in the newly turned earth. She put them in a jar to use as bait the next time they went fishing.

"I want to catch a great big old fish all by myself," she stated firmly.

After a short rest, Charlie took his gun out into the woods. They soon saw him bringing back a big turkey.

"Are you up to cooking more, Evie?" he called. "I have a squirrel here, too."

"I'm always up to cooking, Charlie. I'm really not prepared for a big turkey out here, though."

"Then just leave me some bread and salt; I'll cook the squirrel myself and spend the night here. You take the turkey home for your supper, and have Earl bring me a plate of food when he comes back out tomorrow."

Earl cautioned, "Keep your gun handy, and don't be afraid to use it. You are legally allowed to protect our property. I'll be back before dark and spend the night out here with you."

On the way home in the wagon, while Amy napped in the back, Earl talked seriously to Evie. "You know Charlie is like the son I always wanted."

Evie nodded.

"I had a long talk with him about Thelma. He said her husband was killed in an accident in New River. They had already bought the property here and had plans to improve it. She was devastated when he died. She had a small baby to raise and her mother was dead."

"I thought maybe she was widowed. Charlie mentioned that he'd noticed that her father's last name was Miller and hers was Dubarry," Evie nodded.

"Yes. Her father came here to stay with her to help out, but her little house isn't big enough for the three of them."

"I know that Charlie's been going up to see her."

"He likes her a lot, and he adores her little boy."

"Oh, Earl, I hope we don't lose Charlie to Thelma."

"I hope so too, but we likely will, Evie. We might as well face it."

****

As soon as the Brown's wagon was out of sight on the road to Norma, a buggy drove into The Clearing.

Rube and Thelma called a greeting to Charlie and he went over to help them down.

"We wanted to see the place," Rube explained. When Rube got down from the seat Charlie noticed the older man had a slight limp but was without crutches. He helped Thelma lift the basket that held Matthew.

"How are you, Charlie?" asked Thelma.

"I'm good as new," Charlie replied as he carried Matthew to the cabin and set the basket on the flat stone step, dropping down to sit beside it.

"It looks like you're on the mend, Rube. Could you bring out a couple of chairs?"

"Yep. Better every day." Rube brought out the chairs, setting one up for his daughter and sitting in the other.

"I've got a squirrel ready to go into the pot, Thelma, if you don't mind shoving it in with a little salt. Then we'll talk."

"Papa and I will be going to his place in New River soon. We want to see what kind of shape his old house is in after the winter."

"Do you know how long you'll be gone?"

Rube answered, "We're thinking Thelma might as well put her place up for sale and live with me. My place is bigger."

"We want to have a big garden and some chickens," said Thelma. "And some geese," Rube added. "I want feathers for pillows and such."

"Is your place right on the river?"

"No. It's in the town of New River. We're a good way from the water. I only have about two acres. My brother and his family live close by. They've been keeping an eye on the place for me."

When the baby started to fuss a little, Charlie picked him up. "Does he look like his father?"

"Yes, and his grandmother too," answered Thelma.

"He's growing fast. I'll miss him. Both of you, too."

"Come see us soon," said Rube, "and stay the weekend. There's plenty of room. I'll draw you a map so you can find it easily. Well, I guess we'd better be going."

"Before we leave, though, can you come out to my place?" Thelma asked. "I'll fix dinner for you on Sunday, if you'd like."

"That sounds fine. I'll be there."

Charlie carried Matthew to the buggy with them, and kissed him on the cheek.

"See you Sunday, then." Thelma waved goodbye as they drove down the lane.

****

When Earl rode back in from town that evening, he put his horse in the new shed, then walked over to Charlie. "I heard some news while I was home. A Mr. Kincaid has opened a brickyard on the road to Huntsville. He'll be hiring next Monday. The pay is more than I can pay you. I know you're planning on marrying Thelma and I'm going to lose you anyway. Do you want to go and apply for one of the jobs?"

"Well, tell me more about it."

"All I know is, he makes bricks from clay and has a kiln to fire them. He'll only be running during the summer and early fall, weather permitting, resuming in the spring."

"I sure would like to add to my bank account," said Charlie. "If you're sure you don't mind me leaving you." He stopped and scratched his head. "But wait – how do you know I'm going to ask Thelma to marry me?"

Earl laughed. "Oh, we can see the signs, all right." He reached over and patted the young man on the shoulder. You know you're the son I never had. I want the best for you, and I feel that Thelma will make you happy. But you need a more substantial job."

Early Monday morning Charlie rode to the place where Mr. Kincaid was hiring, and joined the small crowd that had gathered there. He noticed that he was the youngest man in the group. "I can do this," he thought.

The owner interviewed him and was impressed with his determination. "I think you'll do just fine. See my foreman at the next table."

Charlie left, feeling very proud, and went to Earl's house to pack his things.

James Beal

One afternoon, sitting at Evie's table and sipping a glass of tea, Kathy mentioned a young boy who had begun to work for Paul. "One day he showed up at the store while Paul was there shopping. He said his name was James Beal and he wanted work; said he was very unhappy at home. His real father died a long time ago, but his mother remarried and now they live with a stepfather who can be violent."

"How old is he?"

"He's only 14. Paul felt sorry for him, and promised him a small wage. Then he persuaded my father to let the boy stay at his house if he would agree to go to school every day with my little sisters."

"Does he have any other family?"

"Only one older sister, I think he said her name is Carrie. James told Paul that she is unhappy with the stepfather, too. He said he tried to get her to come to Norma with him, but she wouldn't leave her mother."

"I'm glad Paul stepped in; and your pa, too. He sounds like a boy who needs someone on his side," said Evie.

****

James Beal was at school one bright and sunny day, playing outside with his new friends at recess, when he suddenly froze in his tracks and stood staring at a man sitting in an old wagon just off the school grounds. It was his stepfather. He ran immediately into the school building but the man followed him right up to the teacher's desk.

Mr. Grimes looked up at once from his papers. "What's the problem?" he asked.

"This is my son, and I have come to take him home."

"No! He IS NOT my father. He's only my stepfather," said James.

The stern looking man ignored the boy. "He ran away from home and I'm taking him back. Get your things, James."

"I don't want to go. I'm working for Paul Redmond now, and I want to stay in Norma."

The teacher said kindly, "James, if this is your stepfather, I can't stop him. He has the right to take you home."

Malinda, Dora and Hallie Lawson stood on the playground and watched the man roughly shove their new friend into the wagon and drive off out of sight.

"Tell Teacher I've gone home," Malinda called over her shoulder as she took off running as fast as she could to tell her father what had happened.

****

After supper, Sam, Paul and Kathy sat in the living room, quietly discussing the situation. Sam gazed into the fire and said quietly, "Paul, as far as I can see, our hands are tied. What can we do?"

"I for one want to go up there and get James, his sister, and his mother and bring them here."

Sam said, "You know you can't do that. There are laws."

"Well, we can take the law with us."

Kathy stood, saying, "I'll leave you two to sort it out. I have work to do." She stopped and added, "But I'd like for you to go get them, too."

Sam said, "Come home with me, Paul. I have to go feed and milk, and we can talk some more."

Sherriff Wade sat in his office the next morning, smoking his pipe and listening intently to Sam and Paul.

"What harm can it do to go up and talk to Mrs. Allerton and ask her if she wants to leave?"

"Yes, we could go up for just a friendly visit," the sheriff nodded. "Not officially, you understand. We can just talk to the woman and find out more of the facts. Let's plan to go up there tomorrow."

The two friends left with hope in their hearts, and they all slept better that night.

Amelia and Carrie Beal

Amelia was concerned about Carrie. All morning she had cried as she was doing her chores. When Amelia asked what was wrong her daughter just kept sweeping the floor and wouldn't talk. Amelia left her in the house and went to gather eggs and feed the chickens and her dog. She really missed the cow that had provided milk and butter for her family. Bob had taken it one day and she hadn't been able to stop him. She supposed he had sold it.

She regretted marrying Bob Allerton. She'd been lonely since her first husband had died, and she could barely make ends meet. Then Bob came along, and he had been so good to her children, winning their hearts as well as her own. He promised many things if she would agree to marry him. She trusted him and took him into her home, and they were happy for a while. Then things changed. He grew critical and harsh. Nothing pleased him, and he would leave for days with no explanation.

He always came back, apologetic and promising to do better; but the cycle continued.

Amelia was no match for her husband when he was angry. She was half his size, and Carrie was terrified of him. James was too young to stand up to his stepdad, and even when he had managed to run away, Bob had brought him back. She felt so helpless and alone. All her relatives had passed away, and her friends were in Knox County and too far away to help her.

She was hanging wet towels on the clothes line behind her house, when she was startled by voices and the sound of horses coming up the little lane. She hurried around to the front in time to see two men enter her yard.

The first man spoke: "Ma'am, I'm Sheriff Wade and this is Paul Redmond. We've brought James' horse home. Is he around?"

"No, not at the moment. He's down on Buffalo Creek, fishing."

"May we speak to you for a few minutes?"

"Yes. Come inside."

Paul and the sheriff stepped inside the house.

"Please sit down. May I offer you a drink of water?" Amelia was frightened, but struggled to be gracious to her unexpected guests. She wondered what trouble her husband had gotten himself into now.

Carrie came quietly into the room, and Amelia introduced her.

"Carrie, these men brought James' horse back," she explained.

Sherriff Wade took a seat and began, "Mrs. Allerton, I've heard that you're not altogether safe here on Brimstone Mountain."

She did not immediately respond, so Paul explained, "Your son has been staying at the home of Sam Lawson, in Norma, and he's told Sam about your situation."

Amelia stared coldly at the sheriff. "My son did not have permission to discuss private matters with strangers."

"He's only concerned for your safety, Mrs. Allerton."

Paul said kindly, "Mrs. Allerton, has your husband ever struck you or your daughter?"

Amelia began to cry and Carrie went to her and put her hand on her mother's shoulder.

"I'll answer you, Mr. Redmond," she said bravely. "Yes, my stepfather is a violent man sometimes. He has beaten both my mother and me. My brother has told you the truth. James ran away because he could not defend himself from Bob."

Sheriff Wade asked, "Mrs. Alleerton, would you consider leaving him and making a statement about his abuse?"

"No. I cannot. I have nowhere to go. I have two children and I'm unable to do anything." Amelia put her hands to her face and continued to weep quietly.

"You are not helpless, Mrs. Allerton," said the Sheriff. "You have friends. Paul here and his father-in-law have told me they would gladly have all three of you visit them."

Paul nodded, and added, "Your daughter should not be at the mercy of this man. Think of her."

Carrie said, "Mama, listen to these men. I'm going to go get James from the creek right now. I'll work wherever I can to get away from here."

The girl ran outside, called to her dog, and ran down the trail into the trees.

"I'll go with you, Mr. Redmond, for the sake of my children; but I insist on working to earn our keep until I can make other plans."

"Of course, Mrs. Allerton. Would you like us to step out while you pack a few things?"

An hour later, Carrie and her mother rode on James' horse with loaded saddlebags. James rode with Paul, and the small family left Brimstone Mountain behind.

Amelia sighed as she clung to Carrie's waist. "I can't believe we are really doing this."

"I'm glad we are. Bob has hurt you for the last time."

"He'll find us."

"He might, Mama, but he can't hurt us. We have friends now, and the Sheriff is on our side, remember?"

"We have to go back for the dog, Carrie. And what about the chickens? Bob won't feed them; they'll starve."

"We'll go back, Mama, and take care of things soon. We'll work something out with the Sheriff. Don't worry your head about it. Just be glad we're getting away from there."

****

Kathy saw them coming. "Come quick, Papa! It's Paul and he's got James with him!" She looked again, and added, " and it looks like his mother and sister, too!"

The supper table was crowded that night. Kathy liked Amelia and Carrie at once, and James was happier than he had ever been. He went with Sam to do the evening chores, and kept promising all sorts of things he would do for him and Paul.

"I'm glad we have your family as our guests, son. Let's just relax and enjoy it."

Lydia heard about James and his family coming to the Lawson house, and sent Will to invite them to dinner on Sunday after church.

Amelia was shy at first but soon warmed to Lydia and Jasmine. She talked at length to her new friends over the next weeks about her options. At their urging, she notified Bob that she wasn't coming back, and he was furious. She managed to remove her personal belongings from her property, and brought the dog to the Lawson home.

Amelia was pleased to be able to make herself useful around the Redmond household, and Kathy was happy to have the help for she found herself tiring easily late in her pregnancy.

Carrie blossomed in her new surroundings and easily made friends with Kathy's younger sisters. The family treated her to cake and canned peaches for her sixteenth birthday, and Dora cut her curly hair into a style she loved.

"Kathy, do you suppose Carrie could come stay with Andrew and me to help out? I'm miserable with this pregnancy. She could stay in our extra room." Stella wiped her hand across her brow in emphasis.

Kathy was enthusiastic about the idea. "I'm sure she'd love to make some extra money."

Carrie was a good cook and learned to be a good housekeeper as well. Stella was pleased to have her help.

Thelma Dubarry and Reuben Miller

When Thelma and her father made the long trip to their old home in New River, they found the house in sad shape. The roof leaked and weeds had taken over the garden space. The barn was in fair shape, however, and they put the team up there to rest. The two were glad to have dinner that evening with Rueben's family.

"You need to do a few things before you can sleep over there," said his sister-in-law, Lillian. "You should spend the night here with us."

Both were tired, so they gratefully accepted.

Morning found them rested and ready to begin work.

Lillian offered to keep little Matthew for the day, and maybe the next day too, so Thelma could work freely. He was old enough now to drink milk from a glass and eat soft foods, so Thelma felt it was all right to allow him to stay.

Rube rested his knee often, but worked steadily all morning clearing away growth from the porch and windows while Thelma cleaned the floor. Rube checked the chimney for the first fire to heat water, and found it satisfactory, so they were able to enjoy a short tea break before they continued their labors.

At mid-day they stopped to eat a cold meal, and took water and oats to the horses. After a short rest, Rube brought one of the beds into the front room and stripped it and scoured the bedstead. Thelma had brought bedding in the wagon. She put fresh sheets on the bed and hung the pillows outside to air.

After another restful night at Lillian's, the next morning it rained. "Well, now I know where the leaks are," Rube commented wryly as he placed bowls and pans under each drip "I'll sure need some help getting that roof fixed," he continued.

The window was streaming with dark streaks as the rain mixed with the dirt. "It'll take a while to get these windows clean," added Thelma.

They had brought Matthew with them that day, and she stopped to change him, and put him down for his nap. "Maybe we can sleep here tonight," she said.

"I'd like that," said Rube. "I feel better in my own place."

They lit kerosene lamps and ate supper with the good feeling that now they were home. As Thelma prepared for bed she wondered what Charlie was doing and when he would come to see them.

Little Matthew was already asleep when she climbed into bed. She soon joined his gentle snoring.

Annabel and Buck Tarwater

Charlie's mother Annabel was cooking at her stove when Buck came charging in. "Is supper ready?"

"Not quite. I'm in the middle of fixing it."

"Well, I'm hungry now!" He slammed a chair against the wall.

"I never know when you're coming in," said Annabel, trying not to flinch.

Ben came inside, and when he saw his father's angry face he hurried to stand between his parents. Buck towered over him.

"Get out of my way," Buck growled, picking up another chair. When Ben did not move, Buck backed off just a little. "Well, hurry it up," he said, slamming the chair back down onto the floor.

That night Ben heard his mother crying. He felt so helpless. He and his brother Bo were not strong enough to fight their father, who forced them to work at the still, chopping wood to feed the fire and filling fruit jars with moonshine. They weren't allowed to attend school. Annabel had taught them the alphabet and numbers, and they had read some on their own, but both knew they were far behind others their age. He whispered to Bo, "I wish we could get away like Charlie did."

"Be quiet, Ben, if he hears us there'll be trouble for sure."

Morning came. Roosters crowed and cool breezes wafted from the north. Buck was up early. "Get up, Annabel, and fix me some eggs," he yelled. "Boys, get your clothes on. Now! We gotta get out to the still."

Annabel jerked awake, reached for her wrapper, and climbed out of bed. She had not rested enough but she knew she had to get up and fry eggs for Buck. There was not enough flour for hoecakes, so she used it to make some quick bread instead.

The boys put on their boots and came to the kitchen. "Don't frown like that, Ben," Bo said. "You know that moonshine still pays good money. We have lots of work to do today."

Ben looked helplessly at the floor. He hated the still, but knew he couldn't say anything while Buck was around. He knew Bo hated it too, and just wouldn't admit it.

The three gulped their skimpy breakfast and set off into the woods behind the barn.

Annabel boiled several eggs and drank the last of the coffee. "Buck will be furious when he finds out there's no more in the cupboard," she thought. "Even though he hasn't bought any food for a long time, he'll still be mad at me."

She didn't cry. She was very solemn. She put on her best dress and put a few personal things into a pillowcase. She carried it out to the barn and saddled one of the horses. She put the case in a saddlebag, then mounted the gentle mare.

She was leaving Buck. He had been such a handsome and loving man back when they were young. When they lived in Georgia, they were very happy. But he had gotten into a loud argument with his boss and was fired. His uncle had built a house in the East Tennessee mountains, but had then moved back to Atlanta. He went to his uncle and bought the now vacant house and land without asking Annabel, then announced that they were leaving for Tennessee immediately.

Annabel thought of all this while she rode down the trail to the foothills of Brimstone. She would find Charlie and get help. He had wanted her to leave the mountain when he did, and now she had made up her mind to do so. Charlie would take care of her.

Kathy Redmond

At the Lawson Place the gardens were green with vegetables and the apple and pear trees were bearing fruit. Kathy wanted to begin canning, but was unable to do much of anything. She was clumsy and felt uncomfortable all the time.

Paul had been working at the grist mill and her papa was busy in the fields. Since school was out for the summer, James was very useful helping Sam with the bees and the corn, and he hoed the watermelon patch. Dora and Amelia canned tomatoes and made green tomato pickles, and Hallie and Malinda peeled potatoes and onions for soups and other dishes for the table. Kathy sat watching all of them work, and felt very useless. She thought, "Mama went through this five times, and I never heard her complain. I have a great respect for her."

Bob Allerton

One day Sheriff Wade arrived at the Lawson home, asking to speak to Amelia. "I have some news for you, Mrs. Allerton. Your husband was found yesterday on the bank of Buffalo Creek. He was dead."

"Oh!" Amelia's eyes opened wide and her hand flew to her mouth. She found her way to a chair and sat down abruptly. Dora brought her a cup of water and sat beside her, holding her hand.

"We took him up to the house in Brimstone. You need to go up to make funeral arrangements. Afterward you can move yourself and your family back onto the place."

That night Amelia had mixed emotions about her husband. She had not wanted him dead, and yet at the same time she felt a welcome release of the terrible tension she had been feeling for the past number of years.

"I can't help feeling a little bit relieved," she confessed guiltily to her daughter.

Carrie reassured her, saying, "Mama, don't feel bad. You did what you could. He was just no good. He drank himself to death." Earnestly, she reached for her mother's hand. "Now you can get rid of that place. Please sell it. We never have to live there again."

Sam Lawson drove the Amelia and the children up Brimstone Mountain the next day. He helped Amelia arrange for a grave to be dug near the woods and for a minister to come and say a few words. A few neighbors came to say some kind words to Amelia while the dirt was put down over the casket. They had each brought a dish to share afterward as was customary after funerals.

Later several neighbors from Norma came up and repaired the worst damage that Bob had done to the house in his drunken rages. Amelia was grateful to them, and did not know how to begin to thank them for their many kindnesses.

Amelia found the deed the next week and immediately put the property on the market. She had no desire to remain on the mountain. She sold two horses and used the money to rent a room at the boarding house in Norma. Taking only a few of her favorite items with her, she settled in there to rest and wait for her property to sell.

Carrie went back to work for Stella at the Harness' house and James continued to stay with Sam and work on the Lawson farm. They were delighted to say goodbye to the dilapidated house and barn. Both had fully adjusted to living in Norma.

Sam Lawson was there every time Amelia needed a shoulder to cry on. Her daughter was delighted that the two had become close, and James practically worshipped the kind and caring older man.

Summertime

When it was time for Kathy to have her baby, Amelia went back to the Lawsons' to help. Paul was so proud when he became a father, and Sam strutted with pride when they told him they had named their baby boy Samuel Paul Redmond.

All the neighbors came to see Sammy, as the new baby was to be called, and brought knitted shirts and blankets and other gifts. Amy was allowed to hold the baby ... with help from Evie ... and she felt very proud.

Will and Lydia had visits from Dent and Dee, and Caroline came home for the summer, too. Kirby and Molly Lee drove to Norma to see Sammy, and Martha came home for a weekend as well. They all met at Will's house one Sunday afternoon to sing and dance. Jasmine and Silas played and sang for them. Maggie Creech came for a short time with Lenora and Frank, and enjoyed watching the younger couples dancing.

Rueben's Place in New River

Rueben and Thelma had spent long hours repairing his house in New River. Rube's brother and two of his nephews had come to help clear the land. They planted some late beans and some sweet corn.

One Saturday, as Thelma was feeding Matthew, she heard a shout from outside and ran to the door. Charlie had driven into the yard and when he jumped down from the wagon seat Thelma ran into his arms, unashamed of her emotions. He held her for a long minute.

"I brought a few things you might need," he said simply.

Once the horses were cared for Charlie settled down to tell them all the news in Norma, which took quite a while, as he sat contentedly with Matthew on his knee.

There was plenty to do at the farm. Rube showed Charlie the patch where the late beans and corn grew steadily. "We'll plant some pumpkin and squash seeds, and by the time the beans and corn are harvested, the pumpkins can spread out; later, I'll plant turnips. Both of us like turnip greens and they can stretch out many a meal."

After dinner, Rube and Charlie went hunting. While they were out, they assessed Rube's property. They were pleased to find muskedines and other wild grapes which would ripen in the heat of the summer. Hickory, oak, and white walnut grew in abundance. Trout and the native buffalo fish swam in the stream that flowed down on the west side of the woods. Both red and sugar maples grew near the stream, with bloodroot, ginseng and other herbs on the forest floor.

"Take note of these, Rube, so you can return in the fall and sack up some. Andrew Harness at the general store will gladly buy them from you."

Charlie saw movement in an oak and took aim. One of the dogs retrieved the squirrel as soon as it fell, and Rube shot another as it ran along a limb.

"There's supper," he said, simply.

The Allerton Farm

One Saturday, when Charlie had some time off from the brick factory, he picked up Sam and Paul, and drove them in the buggy up to the Allerton farm, where they met up with Amelia and Carrie and James. The men took hoes and other tools, and Carrie and Amelia carried baskets of food for a picnic in the yard.

Everyone worked to clean up the place and make it presentable for sale. They raked out weeds and burned trash and cleaned the little house before they sat down to have a picnic. James brought fresh water from the cold spring.

Carrie said she wanted to dig up some rose bushes to take back to Norma; Sam said she could plant them at his place until she and her family had a place of their own.

James went to the creek and caught two large buffalo fish which they fried over a campfire.

James said, "I hope this place sells soon."

"So do I," said Carrie. "I want us to get a place of our own so our family can all be together."

Luckily their wishes were granted when the pastor of the local church came by and said, "I've been interested in this land since I conducted your husband's funeral here. I can offer you $100 as a down payment, and pay the rest with monthly installments."

Amelia agreed on an amount, and all was settled. Her eyes shone with joy. "You have made me so happy."

****

Sam knew from Charlie that Thelma Dubarry's little house out off Jamestown Road was for sale, and he took Amelia and her son to look at it. "I know the place," he explained on the way there. "It's small," he continued, "but you might buy some of the adjoining land later on."

As soon as they arrived, James looked around and said angrily, "This house is no more than a shack."

"Yes, I know, Son. I suppose we could enlarge it."

"The shed is falling down and there's no barn. I don't like it, Mama."

"There's some fine timber on this land, and there's a nice stream running through it. See those walnuts and locusts? They would shade the west side. You could add a room." Sam was more enthusiastic than the other two. "You could at least talk to the owners, Amelia."

She agreed. "I think I would like it, Sam, if we can fix it up." She turned to James, saying, "And you will too, Son, once you see how good we can make it look."

James was quiet all the way back to the Lawson home, and as soon as the wagon stopped he jumped down and ran to the barn to be alone.

"He's upset, Sam. What should I do?"

"Give him some time. I think I know what the problem is. He's gotten very attached to Paul and this house. He dreads leaving here. Be patient. I think he will come around."

"I hope you're right. Thank you for being such a big help to me."

"Stay the night here again, and let him come in when he's ready."

Caroline

Caroline came home for the summer. She was free until September, when she would go back to school in Knoxville.

She had been out gathering blackberries and picking green beans, and had taken her little sister and brother to the creek to teach them to swim. but finally Lydia said, "I need Nancy and Mike to pick tomatoes for me to can, Caroline. Fun time is over until Saturday."

Feeling bored, she sought her father. "I really should go back to the city and get a job to help out on some of my expenses, Papa. I can stay here all summer but it won't pay for my tuition."

"I don't want you staying alone in Knoxville, Caroline," said Will firmly. "You are safe at the college but I would worry too much if you were living off campus."

"If I just do housekeeping here, it won't be enough to make a difference, Papa," She pleaded. She did not want to admit to him that she missed Eli Greene, whom she had been seeing since they had both returned to Knoxville after the Christmas holidays.

"Let's give it some thought, Caroline. Stay here and help out for a while, anyway."

Amelia's New House

On the Fourth of July there was a big celebration in Huntsville, on the other side of Scott County. People drove in to listen to speeches, to meet their friends, and to picnic on quilts spread on the grass. They came on horseback, in buggies and in wagons, to enjoy the watermelon and lemonade provided by the mayor. Politicians spoke in front of the courthouse, men sat and discussed the issues, and women tended their babies and chatted among themselves.

Sam took Amelia to enjoy the festivities, and on the way home they drove out to see Thelma's Dubarry's little house out off Jamestown Road. They liked what they saw, and Sam suggested strongly that they see about buying it.

The next Monday Sam and Amelia drove down to New River. It was almost dark when they arrived at the home of Reuben Miller and his daughter Thelma

Dubarry. Their house sat back from the road with a long yard. Sam had not expected the trip to take this long.

"Hello, Mr. Miller." Sam tipped his hat. "It's good to see you again. We've been out to see Thelma's land near the Jamestown Road, and we understand you might be interested in selling it."

Rube said, "Yes; Thelma has decided to move here with me. We can't keep up with both houses."

Amelia said. "We liked the property – at least what we saw of it last week. It's sort of isolated, though, and I'm used to neighbors. Since I have two teen-aged children, they may not be happy there. So, would it be possible to rent it with an option to buy?"

Thelma said, "We have had no other offers, so I suppose we could consider it."

They discussed terms and came to an agreement.

Sam explained, "We didn't calculate the miles correctly, so we'll have to spend the night here in New River. Do you know of a boarding house or inn nearby where we might get rooms?"

Reuben answered, "Not any close enough to reach before dark, but you're welcome to stay here overnight."

Thelma agreed, "You are most welcome. We're just plain country folks and it's common to have strangers spend the night."

Rueben said, "We haven't been here very long so the place isn't as clean as it could be, but I'm sure you'll be comfortable."

"We really appreciate it."

"By the way, have you eaten?"

"No, we came straight on, stopping only for a snack along the way. I'm afraid we didn't plan very well."

"Let's go bed down your horses for the night, while Thelma prepares a meal. I'll lend you a nightshirt to sleep in."

Amelia said, "You're so kind, Thelma. Just anything will do; don't go to any trouble."

"It's no bother at all. I'll just heat up some of the rabbit stew we had for supper. And we have cornpone and milk. We just bought a cow this week and have plenty of milk."

Matthew started to fret and Thelma had to stop and feed him and settle him for the night. Amelia watched the pot of stew, and set out bowls for the adults.

When Sam and Rueben returned, the four sat down to eat and discuss their plans.

Amelia said, "Isn't it exciting to plan your house? That's what Sam and I are doing. We're to be married very soon."

"I'm so happy for you. I'm also to be married. My Charlie is working in Norma right now."

Amelia said, "Let me pay you two months in advance now and you can write out a receipt. We'll be leaving early in the morning."

"I can give you an egg breakfast. We have a few chickens already. I'm afraid it will only be hoe cakes though. I don't have the makings for biscuits."

"That'll be fine. You must visit us in the place when we get it fixed up, Thelma."

The following morning both Sam and Amelia were refreshed and ready for the trip home. Rube went with Sam to feed his stock and fed Sam's team some oats. Thelma walked out with Amelia as they said their goodbyes, and wished them a safe trip.

****

Back at the Lawson house in Norma, Carrie was up before the others. Her mother had not come back last night and she was worried. James got up too, and they walked out to the springhouse together for water.

"Mama's all right, Carrie. You can trust her with Sam. They had to spend the night somewhere. I guess it took longer than they figured."

"I know, James. I just couldn't sleep any longer. I want to know if they bought the land. If they did, we'll have a home. A real home."

"Well, there'd be a lot of work ahead of us."

Carrie said sternly, "I intend to help all I can ... and I expect you to do the same."

James nodded. "Do you think I'll have my very own room, Carrie?"

"I expect so. Have you seen the house plans?"

"No, but I hope it's a real big house with a porch."

"Me, too. Let's go in and start breakfast."

Mr. and Mrs. Sam Lawson

The little Baptist Church at Norma was decorated with roses and other fresh flowers and candles. The seats were all filled, and after the Sunday service the entire congregation stayed to see Pastor Greene conduct the marriage ceremony for Amelia Allerton and Sam Lawson. The bride was radiant, dressed in pale orchid and carrying pink roses. Carrie stood by her mother as maid of honor, dressed in a light blue frilly dress. James was the best man, standing tall and proud.

Sam took Amelia to the inn in Huntsville to spend the night, while her two children stayed with Will and Lydia. After supper at the Wilsons', Will and James discussed the improvements to be made at the new place. "You know, we'll all work together to make it a fine home for your family, James. You'll see."

James nodded, but was not really fully convinced. He still thought the house was too small and rough ... and too far from his friends.

****

The new family drove out to the cabin. They carried picks, shovels, hoes and brooms. Sam and James started to tear down the old shed, piling the wood to be used later to build a hen house. Amelia and Carrie swept out the old cabin and planned where they wanted the front porch and a new window. "I'll show you the plans for the house, and you can see where your room will be," Amelia promised. "Let's go see what the boys are doing."

Amelia and Sam drove into Huntsville for a day. After enjoying a fine dinner at the inn, they went to an auction, where Sam chose a gentle horse and small buggy for Amelia. She was thrilled to drive it Norma, with Sam following behind.

James was delighted when he saw the horse and asked if he could drive the buggy. "Yes, you can drive when we go out to the house again. The horse's name is Pete."

Amelia was glad that James was happy with the buggy. It was a good sign that he was going to accept the new place. At last she was going to have a good man to love her and her two precious children and live with them in their own little house. "I don't deserve such happiness," she thought with a sigh.

Buck, Ben and Bo Tarwater

Earl was happy. Out at The Clearing the cozy cabin was caulked for the winter ahead and his woodworking equipment had been moved to the new shop.

Charlie had gone to New River for a couple of days to visit Thelma, and Earl had gone fishing that morning for a change of pace. He had just returned and cleaned his fish when he saw a horse approaching. He reached for his gun. Then he saw it was a woman riding into the lane.

He rose to help her down.

"I'm looking for Charlie Tarwater. I'm his mother."

"Please sit down, Ma'am. Charlie isn't here at the moment. I'm his friend, Earl Brown."

"When will he be back?"

"Not for a couple of days. He would want me to take care of you, Mrs. Tarwater. Let me give you some coffee."

"I need to talk to Charlie," insisted Annabel. "It's quite urgent."

"Charlie is all the way down in New River. I hope I can help you."

"Mr. Brown, I will not be returning to my house in Brimstone for a while. I have no money for lodging, as I had hoped to find Charlie here."

"Mrs. Tarwater, you are more than welcome to stay with my family in town. We can leave your horse here and I'll take you into Norma. My wife and daughter will be happy to meet you."

Evie greeted Annabel warmly, and they all had a hot meal while Annabel told them of her problems.

"My husband, Buck, may come looking for me. He'll be sure to come to you, Mr. Brown, and with Charlie away, I'm afraid there could be trouble."

"May I be frank? We know about your husband from Charlie. He has wanted you to come to Norma for a long time. Please call me Earl, and this is Evie. We feel like we know you."

"Thank you. Please call me Annabel."

"You're welcome to spend the night with us. Then tomorrow we can decide what to do. It's a long way to New River. Charlie will be back and you can see him then."

The next morning, Earl said, "Annabel, I need to go to The Clearing, and you won't be safe here. I think we ought to take you over to the Wilson's house. They will welcome you and when Charlie comes out to work, I'll tell him where you are."

Evie agreed. "If your husband comes here you and I can't fight him off, but at Will's house you'll be safe."

Annabel agreed that was a good idea.

"I'll take you over there before I leave," Earl added.

Charlie rode into The Clearing the next afternoon and called to Earl.

"Don't get down, Charlie. I have news. Your mother rode down here yesterday looking for you. She's at Will Wilson's house now and I want you to go right over there to see her."

Charlie was astounded, but he quickly recovered.

"I'll go right away," he said.

****

Lydia had made Annabel comfortable and she certainly was sympathetic to her cause. Jasmine came over and everyone tried to make Charlie's mother feel at home.

Annabel fed the chickens and did a few other things to help out. She felt safe with these wonderful people and since Buck didn't know where she was she felt he couldn't harm her.

They spent the next morning getting acquainted and Annabel was content to wait for Charlie. He came in the afternoon.

After they had talked together, Will made a suggestion. "Why don't you continue to stay here while Charlie is working?"

Jasmine spoke up. "She should stay at our house. It is farther from the road and even if her husband comes out here he won't be able to see to our end of the lane."

"Charlie, when you go home on the weekend, you can take her home to New River with you."

Charlie agreed, but asked, "How do you feel about that, Mama?"

"Only if I can cook and be of some help for my keep," answered Annabel.

"Then it's settled," said Jasmine. "You will be our guest."

Silas said. "Don't worry, Charlie, we'll take very good care of her."

Charlie borrowed a wagon the next weekend and brought Annabel to his and Thelma's home. He was worried about his two teenaged brothers still on the mountain working at the still with his father, but perhaps he and his mother could figure out a way to get them safely away, also.

It was a strenuous trip for Annabel. They only stopped once to rest the horses briefly and to eat a snack before they continued riding along, talking of their future plans.

Annabel settled in at her son's house and although worried about Ben and Bo, was content to help Thelma with the house and cooking. For several days she took walks and mended socks and helped with little Matthew.

Rueben and Thelma were in the yard when three riders came galloping along the road, then slowed when they drew near. Rube got his gun and stood ready as the rough looking men rode into the yard.

"I'm looking for my wife," said the large bearded man as the two tall teenagers quietly looked on.

"Sir, I don't know you but there is no one here except my family."

"Is this where Charlie Tarwater lives?"

"It is. He's not at home right now."

The stranger pulled a gun from his belt.

"I'm his pa. If he's in that house, I want him to come out here. Now! "

"Mr. Tarwater, I would appreciate it if you would leave my property. Your folks are not here."

"Boys, go look in the house and see if Charlie or your ma are in there."

Reluctantly, the boys climbed down and went into the house. Returning quickly, one said, "They're not here, Pa."

Rueben glared at the man and once more asked him to leave.

The man said, without turning his head, "did you boys look in the cellar?"

Just then their attention was drawn to the road. Charlie rode into the yard with Annabel. He frowned when he saw his father there.

"Let me help you down, Mama. Don't worry. I'll handle this."

Buck Tarwater rode over toward his wife, "I have come all this way and I am taking you back with me."

"Mama's staying with me, Pa. I don't want any trouble. She's not safe on the mountain with you gone all the time. She's staying here."

Buck climbed down, and still holding his gun, started toward Annabel. Rueben pulled Thelma and Matthew behind him. The little boy began to cry.

"Pa, don't cause any trouble," said Charlie. "Just leave us in peace, please!"

Buck suddenly grabbed Annabel and pulled her toward his horse. She screamed. Buck pulled her in front of him and threatened to shoot.

"Let her go, Pa," said Charlie. "I mean it. Don't hurt her!"

Buck just held on tighter and said, "Keep away, Charlie. She's coming home!"

When he aimed the gun at Charlie, Annabel screamed again and threw up her arm. The gun exploded in her ears as she felt Buck's hold loosen and she saw him fall to the ground. Blood was spurting from his hair, but he lay very still. She ran to the porch hysterically screaming.

"He's dead," announced Charlie. "Thelma, get me a quilt and we'll cover him up. I'll ride to Hugh's and have him go for the sheriff over in town."

Thelma took Annabel and Matthew inside and came back out with an old quilt, handing it to Rueben. Rueben covered the still, quiet body of Buck Tarwater.

The two boys, still on their horses, rode quickly off down the road and out of sight.

"Let them go, Charlie. Come and sit down with me," said Thelma.

A deputy came with Rube's brother and took their statements. "The Sheriff will be here shortly, but it looks like it was self-defense to me."

Rueben said, "This man came here for trouble and he got more than he bargained for."

Sheriff Bolton came, talked to them, and wrote notes in his little book. "We'll take the body with us, Mr. Miller. Get some rest. We'll be in touch with you."

Charlie held Thelma and cried bitterly. She led him inside and sat with him while Reuben comforted Annabel and they both tried to calm her little boy.

"It's all over now. We can put an end to it. It's all a very bad thing but we'll get over it," Reuben told them all.

News traveled quickly to Norma. A man came into Andrew's store the following morning. He said, "Andy, there was a man killed in New River yesterday by the name of Tarwater."

Andrew stopped and stared. "I know a young fellow who works for Earl Brown who's name is Tarwater."

"This was an older man."

"I must get word to Earl. Go over to his place, Luke. Tell him exactly what you've heard, and come right back."

Rube's brother came with his wife Lillian and cared for the family. Little Matthew was put to bed, and Lillian sat with Annabel. Charlie and Thelma went into one of the bedrooms. Rube and his brother sat and discussed the day, and what could be done to help Charlie and Annabel.

Ezra, Rose and Becky Stone

Ezra Stone and his wife, Rose, and their thirteen year old daughter, Rebecca, mostly called Becky, arrived at the Perkins boarding house in Norma; they found it to be primitive, rustic and dull, at least according to Rose.

"Now, Becky, before we go in to lunch, let me caution you that we do not know these simple people. Remember your manners and do not stare at them. They may be sensitive."

"Yes, Mama." Becky sighed.

Ezra said, "I believe I have time for a walk before the midday meal, which may I remind you, Rose, is known here as dinner, and the evening meal is called supper. I'll be back shortly." He walked out to the general store where he met Andrew Harness. "I'm Ezra Stone. I'll be getting mail here. I've come to inquire about some property that has been advertised. The poster said there are two buildings on a small plot of land."

"Yes, that would be the house across the street there, and also the furniture shop next door to it. Both are owned by Earl Brown."

"Where might I find this Mr. Brown? Would he be in his shop?"

"Probably. If he's not, try the house. If he isn't there, he'll be at his new house out Jamestown Road.

"If you should see him, please tell him I would like to see the property, and that I am staying at the Perkins Boarding House."

Charlie, Ben, Bo and Annabel Tarwater

Charlie climbed the mountain to his old home. He was tired. He had a sled borrowed from Earl, as he planned to take his mother's cedar chest down to Earl's house where he had left his wagon.

He was a little surprised to see Ben as he entered the yard, and he could tell his younger brother was just as surprised to see him. A little worried, too. "Don't worry. I've just come to talk to you and Bo. Let's go in the house."

Inside, Charlie noticed there was clutter everywhere and he didn't even want to see the kitchen.

"Mama is staying with me right now, but I'll tell her you're here and let her decide if she wants to come back. So you two need to clean up this place for her sake." Charlie continued sternly, "There's one thing I demand though. You must destroy the still. If you don't, I will tell the sheriff and he will come and arrest you. I'll tell him you came to my house with guns. Both of you are younger than me, and you know I mean what I say."

Ben said defiantly, "We were making a good living out of that still." Then he looked over at his older brother and his shoulders sagged. "But with Papa gone we can't anymore, anyway. We can't get the corn and sugar."

"Destroy it as soon as possible. Mama can't come up here to live if you don't take care of her. I can get you started with a garden. You can trap and find ginseng to sell, and I will help all I can. I had come to take Mama's cedar chest to New River, but I will leave it here for now, and ask her if she wants to move back. She still loves you boys."

"We don't even have any pigs or chickens up here, Charlie."

"I can bring you a couple of chickens and a hog to raise if you promise to clean the place up."

"We need lye soap though to clean with and there's very little food in the kitchen." Ben looked at Bo, then added, "if you bring Mama back we'll take care of her."

Charlie said, "Ben, put on the cleanest shirt you can find and we'll go get a hog and a few chickens. Bo, you sweep this place and bring water to heat while we're gone. Make up the beds and chop some firewood."

****

Charlie rode to Thelma's New River home and called out. Rube was clearing and burning brush and getting the area ready for his bees. Thelma was gathering dry clothes from the clothesline. Annabel came outside when she heard his voice, and Rube hurried to the house. Matthew came running to greet him.

"I'm going to leave my horse here while I rest," he said as he tied him to a tree. "I have some news, Mama."

"Sit down, Son. What is it?"

"Ben and Bo are back at the house on Brimstone. I had a little talk with them. They said if you wanted to come back home they would help you care for the place."

"What about the still? I won't stay there if they're running it. And I can't stop them by myself."

"They promised to destroy the still ... and they also promised to help you clean the house."

Thelma interjected, "You don't have to go back, Annabel. You can stay here as long as you like."

Charlie continued, "I left your cedar chest there, but I can easily bring it when I go back to check on the boys, if you'd rather stay here with us."

"Let me think about it."

"I took Ben to Norma, got him a few chickens and a young hog, and took him back to the mountain. I took some food for them and some soap and things. They promised to work with me on this."

"Do you trust them, Charlie? They were with their father so much."

"Mama, he forced them to work for him."

"I guess I should go back, Charlie. They need me to take care of the house ... and them," said Annabel.

"Now that the decision has been made I plan to ask at the courthouse if the county will widen the road on your property, and finish it all the way into Norma. It's too hard to get in and out like it is now; I could help with the work," Charlie stated.

"Oh, I'd like that too. If there's a road, I can have company up to my house."

"Then we need to choose a day to take you home. First, I have to help Rube get those logs down here. That'll give the boys time to scrub their clothes and clean the place up for you."

****

Ben and Bo worked for days; they worked hard.

Building a fire under an iron pot full of water as they had seen their mother do, they gathered the bed linen and shoved it in. While it was soaking they scrubbed the floors and washed the windows.

They hung the laundry on the clothesline and polished the kitchen stove.

"It makes me wonder how Mama managed all of this and kept us clean and fed," Bo marveled.

"I wish she could see this place now," said Ben. "She's such a little person. How could she have kept it so clean all by herself?"

"Poor Mama."

"I didn't realize how much she did for us," agreed Ben. "If she comes back, I'm sure going to do more around here." He glared sternly at his little brother. "And you are, too."

"We better get those sheets in. It looks like rain."

Just as they brought the laundry basket through the door, it began to rain. The two boys stood on the porch, watching it pour down. "The rain will make the ginseng and bloodroot pop out. Tomorrow let's go hunting and look for ginseng. Charlie said we could sell it at the general store."

"That's a good idea. There are some baskets and bags in the barn that we can use."

After supper Bo said, "I'm tired. Let's go to bed now, and get an early start tomorrow."

As they turned off the lamp and secured the house for the night, the two brothers were still making plans. "When the ground dries, we better dig up the garden and put out those onion sets and cabbage slips that Charlie brought."

"I can't wait till Charlie sees what all we've done."

"He won't know the place."

"I know. Don't it look good?"

The Brown's House and Shop in Norma

While he was shopping at the general store, Earl learned that there was a new arrival in Norma. Andrew told him that the man was an artist and a writer, and he was interested in purchasing Earl's house and shop across the street.

Earl went immediately to the boarding house to meet the fellow. After touring the two buildings, Ezra Stone declared that they would serve his purposes perfectly, and the two men agreed on a price.

"I expect we could be moved out in another couple of days," said Earl. "We've already taken almost everything out to The Clearing."

"Splendid! If you like, we can go over to the bank right now and settle this."

Later, Evie walked across the street with Amy to see Andrew and Stella at the store.

"I came in to get the mail" she announced, "and to tell you that our house is sold. We'll be moving to The Clearing for good by Wednesday."

"That is good news. Go on back and tell Stella," said Andrew. "She's lying down right now. She'll be glad to see you."

Amelia and Sam's New Place

Amelia and Sam worked at their new farm daily and were very satisfied with the progress.

James had shown his skills, and Amelia was very proud of him. They had added a porch, and rooms on the west side were taking shape.

"Oh, Sam, this place is really going to be just what we wanted. It's such a beautiful location. I can hardly wait until we can move out here."

"Soon, Amelia, soon."

Rose Stone and Dora Lawson

Ezra Stone was in the store to buy several items and while he was there ordered a cook stove from the catalog. The rest of their furniture was arriving daily on the train from Knoxville.

"Andrew, my wife isn't accustomed to all this work. We left all her servants in Philadelphia. Do you know of anyone who might be interested in working for her as a helper?"

"Sure, I can probably find someone for you. I'll ask around and get back to you right away."

At dinner Andrew told his wife and Dora about the opportunity.

"Why don't you go and talk to them, Dora? They will pay much more than we can."

"I'm not sure I could please a city lady."

"Talk to her at least; find out what she wants done before you turn it down," Stella encouraged her younger sister.

The next morning, Dora went over to speak to Rose, and found her sweeping her porch.

"Hello. I'm Dora Lawson. I heard you're interested in hiring someone to help in the kitchen. I'd like to talk to you about the job."

"Yes. Come inside won't you? I do need help with the cooking and laundry. I'm not very good at it. I had servants at our home in Philadelphia, you see."

She showed the young woman around her house. Dora was surprised to see that the kitchen was cluttered and many things were sitting out in various spots.

"Mrs. Stone may be a city lady, but she really does need help," she thought.

They discussed the work and the salary; Dora accepted immediately and agreed to start the very next day, glad that she had taken Andrew's advice.

Annabel Comes Home

Annabel rode up to Brimstone with Charlie. It was very late in the day when they arrived. They found the house shining clean, and the stove was polished. The kitchen table was scrubbed and the shelves held clean dishes and pots and pans.

Charlie was very pleased with his brothers. "You have done extra well, boys."

His mother was tired and quickly lay down on the nice clean bed that Ben and Bo had prepared. She went to sleep in her own room exhausted from the ride from New River. Frogs croaked, crickets chirped and the owls hooted in the woods. Annabel slept soundly. She had come home.

The following morning, Ben and Bo proudly showed Charlie their garden. They had burned off the brush, and dug up the soil with a spade. He was happy to see that they had also repaired the chicken coop.

Annabel stood gazing at her garden, then hugged all her sons. "We're going to be a real family now," she said. She immediately gathered eggs and started a large breakfast for all of her boys. She was happier than she had been in years.

Sam and Amelia Lawson's Cabin

Sam and Amelia were finally able to spend the first night in their cabin. They scrubbed and cleaned all day. They swept out the loft, and spread quilts and pillows for a place to sleep. The fresh mountain air was just right for relaxing under the eaves and talking over their plans for tomorrow.

They rose early and made a campfire, cared for the horses, and had a quick breakfast. A neighbor arrived with Amelia's cook stove, its pipes, and several baskets of utensils in his wagon. "I'll go back now for the bed and worktable," he said. "Do you want anything else, Mrs. Lawson?"

"See if you have room for some chairs, as many as you can squeeze in."

"Right. I'll be back as soon as I can."

They were busy bringing in firewood when James arrived on his horse. He called out to them,

"I brought food from Kathy."

"Good. We already had breakfast but we can always eat a fresh biscuit."

While they were still enjoying the biscuits, Carrie rode up and joined them. She brought the news that Stella's twins had been born the night before. "She named them Frederick and Jonathan. You should see Andrew; he's such a proud father!"

Amelia asked, "Is she doing all right while you're away?"

"Oh, yes. Lydia's there; she brought the blankets she had knitted for the babies, and a nightgown she had made for Stella. And Dora has taken some time off from working for Mrs. Stone so she can stay with her sister for a while, too."

Everyone wanted to show Carrie what they had accomplished, and she was excited to see the improvements to the house and yard.

Sam had built a chicken coop and had three hens there. He showed her where the ground had already been marked off for the first room that would be added to the house. "There will be a cellar here, and then the floor will be built over it. There will also be a large kitchen."

"Oh, I'm so glad. We never had a big kitchen. Be sure to put in windows all over the house. I hate dark rooms."

"Your mother said the same, and she wants a large back porch too, so she can work out there in the summer."

Sam's garden was flourishing, although it was scattered between the tree stumps. He told Carrie that they would use anything that grew to maturity and by next year would have burned out all the stumps, and there would be a more uniform garden patch. He showed her where he planned to put some beehives, like the ones he had at his old house.

"You're a very clever man, Sam," said Carrie.

"I had a good teacher. My father was a soldier who was given land for his service in the army. He learned to survive on the land and used those skills to raise his family."

Amelia cooked and did laundry with joy in her heart. She was settling down to a peaceful life in the country.

James

James had begun to show more interest in the farm.

He showed Carrie where he had started a garden, in a little patch near the shed. "I'm putting in some onions and radishes," he explained proudly. "We don't have much time left in the season, but this will be a start."

He liked to explore the woods and hunt. There were many herbs that had grown freely for years, and James learned the kinds that would sell best to the tradesmen at the store.

Paul had shown him how to set traps for beaver and other animals and how to dry the pelts so they could be sold. Some of these brought a goodly sum at the store.

Sam helped him open a bank account so he could learn to manage money. He was proud to see his savings grow, and he wanted even more to succeed.

James also helped fell the trees and strip the branches for logs that would be used for the walls of the new rooms.

Luke occasionally came over and spent the night with him. They slept in the loft, and enjoyed going fishing higher up in the woods.

Earl and Evie in The Clearing

Earl and Evie polished all the windows in the new furniture shop. He finally had all his equipment and he was busier than ever. A few people had seen the signs and had come in to order various pieces. He had cut a large maple tree and had it drying outside in the sun.

Evie had replanted her roses and peonies, and Amy faithfully helped her water them.

"I miss Charlie ever since he went to New River with Thelma and Rueben," said Earl, "but now that Mr. Stone has bought the old house and shop we have a bit of money to spend. If I have more than I can do, I can hire someone else to help me."

The Stones Settle In

The Stones were settling in to their new home in Norma.

Ezra set up his easels in the shop, and made a studio there where he spent many enjoyable hours painting the beautiful scenery he saw every day on his walks in the area.

He also observed the people he met along the way, and he used another corner of the large area to set up a table with all his writing utensils.

He found plenty to write about – including Earl. He had ridden out to The Clearing to ask about having a porch swing made for Rose, and he and Earl chatted about the furniture business. He later wrote an article about it and sent it off to his publisher in Philadelphia, much to Evie and Amy's delight.

Rose was gradually adapting to the different life style. She missed her servants at first, but found Dora to be an able substitute and easy to train to suit her "city lady ways."

She did not complain for she had promised Ezra his year in Norma. She liked the lifestyle they could afford, and knew she was fortunate to have married him.

Their daughter Becky was having an adventure here in this mountain village. She had made a friend of Luke, and they talked often.

Andrew and Stella discussed the new neighbors while they ate dinner. "They'll be good customers," said Andrew. "They seem to have loads of money. Mr. Stone ordered the finest cook stove in my catalog. They buy lots of meat, eggs and milk, and great amounts of vegetables. I think we'll be ordering a lot more things for our store."

Stella finished the dishes and sat with Freddie on her lap. "Things are working out well for everyone, aren't they? You should see what Mama and Sam have done at the new place. When the babies are older, I will want to go there to live for a while and help Mama out. She'll be cooking for the workers who come to help Sam with logs and heavy work."

Andrew said, "Some Sunday we'll drive out there to say hello and I can see the progress for myself."

The Tarwaters Settle In

Annabel made new curtains for her parlor and two bedrooms. She had Ben clean out the loft so she could store some things up there. Her two younger sons had continued to plant more in the garden and to tend it faithfully. They hunted and fished and sold ginseng at the store. Annabel tutored them both from books she borrowed from the school, and their education improved immensely.

She wrote to her friends in Atlanta and Marietta, Georgia. She could now be proud to write about her family and home.

Charlie, Thelma and Rueben all corresponded from New River, so she was able to keep up with their news and they could keep up with hers.

One day Annabel saw a drawing on a scrap piece of wrapping paper that Ben had left around the house, and she mentioned it to him.

"I just enjoy drawing for fun," he said.

"This is very good, Son. Let me see some others."

She saw that the others were even better. "Here, Ben, use some of my writing paper, and draw some more. I have a good friend from school in Atlanta; his name is Robert Ingress and he's an artist. I would like to send a few of these to him to get his opinion."

The Stones Attend Sam's Roof Raising

On Sunday, Andrew and Stella drove out see how Sam and Amelia were coming along on the renovations to their house. They took their little twin sons, snug in travel baskets, and Luke, carrying another basket filled with fried chicken as a gift for Amelia.

Carrie rushed out and hugged Stella. "I've missed you so," she said. "Come on in to the kitchen. I'll get some chairs. Mama, look who's come to see us!"

"How very nice," said Amelia. "I'm afraid it's very hot in here. I'm cooking dinner."

Carrie took the basket of chicken and said, "Let's leave this here on the table and take our chairs out in the shade. I'll tell Sam and James you're here."

Sam and James showed Andrew and Luke all over the property, and told them the plans for the house. There were logs lying in the back yard and tools here and there.

"It looks great, Sam," exclaimed Andrew. "You've really been busy."

Luke and James went off by themselves and Sam sat with his visitors in the shade of an elm tree. Stella held Freddie on her lap, while his brother continued to sleep in his little basket.

"They are such beautiful babies," Amelia exclaimed.

Stella beamed. "Oh! And guess what? Kathy told me she's expecting another baby!"

Sam looked up, smiling, and said, "I didn't know that!"

"She just told me yesterday," said Stella. "You haven't been home for a while, Papa."

"I'm so pleased to hear it. It's a nice surprise." He rose, saying, "you must stay for dinner. I'll go help Amelia. We can eat out here in the cool. It's too hot inside. We'll soon have a dining room in the house, if I can possibly arrange it. Then, if we need an extra bedroom, we can put a bed in there temporarily. Then the next time you come we can put you up overnight."

"You sure are thinking ahead," said Andrew.

After they had eaten and the babies were asleep again, Amelia showed Stella around the outside of the house. A big chimney made with rock and clay from the river was going up on the western wall. In the edge of the woods there was a chicken coop with a fenced in run. A wire clothesline was nailed to trees and a few towels hung there drying in the sun.

"If you like, I can send some rose cuttings out by Luke one day when he's coming to visit James," offered Stella.

"I would love that. Carrie planted some roses at Sam's house from Brimstone that she plans to take cuttings from for me, too; and some white peonies as well."

Andrew interrupted, "We'd better be going home. It'll be dark soon." He gave a loud whistle, and Luke answered from somewhere in the woods. Both boys came running and Andrew said, "Grab a chicken leg to take with you Luke, we're leaving."

He set the babies' baskets in the buggy and Luke climbed up beside them.

"Please come again, and soon," invited Sam.

"Yeah, Andy, I want to come back and help James build a tree house sometime," said Luke, chewing on a drumstick.

****

A few days later, Andrew went to see Ezra.

"We're going to get together at Sam's house next Saturday and help put the roof on the new addition to his house in the country. We want to invite you and Mrs. Stone to come. We want to show you how mountain people help each other and party at the same time."

"I think I would like to see that. I'll tell Rose. What time should we be there? "

"Most of us arrive at dawn. Come when it's convenient for you, and plan to stay all day. There'll be food, with music and square dancing after the work is done."

That same day Rose and Becky had gone to the store for fresh eggs and Stella was in the post office room. She waved to them, and Rose went back to pick up their mail.

"I hope you're coming next Saturday to the roof raising," she said. "And don't forget to wear a poke bonnet."

"What's a poke bonnet?" asked Becky.

"It's a cloth bonnet with a starched stiff brim to protect you from the sun," said Stella. "You'll see many of them."

"Oh, my," said Rose. "It all sounds very interesting. We'll be looking forward to it."

****

At their new place on Saturday, Amelia and Sam welcomed their friends and neighbors. They had borrowed chairs and quilts to spread on the ground for extra seating. Rose Stone was invited to sit in a cane-bottomed rocker while Ezra walked among the people; observing, getting acquainted, and discreetly taking notes. He spoke to James who filled him in on being the stepson of Sam Lawson. James pointed out his sister, Carrie, who was serving sweet cider to the guests, and told Ezra about Sam's five daughters from his first marriage: Kathy, Stella, Malinda, Dora, and Hallie, who were all there. Later he introduced the writer to Paul Redmond, Kathy's husband.

"My story is a long one, Mr. Stone. When you have time, I'll tell it to you."

"I'll look forward to it, Paul. Please introduce me to your lovely wife and sisters-in-law."

Meanwhile, Lydia Wilson chatted with Rose. "Are you settled in, Mrs. Stone?"

"Just barely, I'm afraid. We have the basics, but more pieces are arriving constantly. It's an enormous undertaking putting a house together." She fanned vigorously as she watched Becky talking with Luke under an oak tree.

Amelia brought a chair and joined them. "I suppose all this is very strange to you, Mrs. Stone."

"Please! My name is Rose. I get very tired of 'Mrs. Stone.' Yes, I do find it very different to see neighbors banding together to help build a man's house."

"It's very common here, Rose. You see, they exchange work with one another. Next month another neighbor may need a helping hand, and the ladies get together and prepare the food and visit. Each one brings a dish, or a jug of something to drink - sweet cider or tea. When the men finish or want to take a break, we eat at those tables under the trees, and it's a good opportunity for all to visit and get caught up on the news."

"A very charming custom. Do you mind telling me where you're from, Amelia? I sense you weren't brought up in these hills."

"Actually I was married in Atlanta. My first husband inherited a small sum, and bought some property on

Brimstone Mountain, a few miles from here. We raised our two children there. That's my son, James, over there splitting shingles, and my daughter, Carrie, is in the checked apron serving at the first table. My first husband is now dead," she added, before Rose could ask.

"Do you ever miss your Atlanta home?"

"No, not at all. I have good friends here. After my husband died, these people were very kind to me."

"Remarkable, my dear. And now you have this new husband and this house going up here."

"Yes, Sam and I were friends from the first time we saw each other. He was a widower with five daughters and was lonely for companionship; the kind we experience now. His family was very approving of our marriage. What about you, Rose?"

"I'm from a military family. I married a struggling writer and we barely survived until his first poems were published. Then we began to prosper."

"I'm so glad. I hope you'll like it here in Norma."

"It certainly is a tight knit community. Ezra seems quite taken with it. Rebecca is adjusting well, too. I see she is making more friends today."

Rose nodded toward Luke and Hallie Lawson.

"That's Sam's youngest daughter. Her name is Hallie. The boy is Andrew Harness' nephew, Luke, who lives with him and Stella."

"I expect Becky will want a poke bonnet like the other girls have."

"They make their own, Mrs. Stone; I mean, Rose. They are quite simple to sew."

"Here comes Ezra now," said Rose. "He looks like he's heading for the cold cider."

****

That night Rose wrote to her sons, who were still living in Philadelphia:

Dear Jeffrey and Thomas,

It was a different kind of day for your father, Rebecca and me. We met the villagers at a working / social gathering which seems to be quite common here in the mountains. They met to put a roof on a house. While the men did the actual labor, the women prepared a picnic on temporary tables, and visited with each other while caring for their babies and small children, and sharing all the neighborhood news.

I met a distinguished lady from Atlanta, who for the love of her husband tolerated the rustic life here and raised two children. She seems very happy. I met others who have changed their circumstances for a productive life here.

I suspect your father will find much grist for his writing mill. As I watched him among the men, he seemed to be enjoying himself immensely, and making more acquaintances as he goes along. I, also, passed the time somewhat pleasantly, and enjoyed the food they served. I must say the climate agrees with me.

Rebecca is making the most of every day, meeting new friends of her own age, and adapting well to the customs. When we return to a more civilized society, I doubt the experience will have harmed her in any way.

Please write often and don't forget to send the newspapers.

Your loving mother.

Ezra added a note of his own.

Dear Jeff and Tom,

We are partially settled in our new cabin. It is not completely furnished. I am more than happy with the experiment and the changes in environment and have made notes on my next project. The people are friendly, helpful, and happy to communicate. I anticipate a successful book, and have also finished several poems and many paintings.

I enjoy the scenery, the customs, and the climate of this remarkable part of the country. Continue to write often. Please pass this letter on to your brother and tell him I expect a long letter from him soon.

Papa

Robert Ingress and Ben Tarwater

Annabel was beating dust from a rug outside on the porch banister, when she heard a sound and turned. A rider was coming up the trail. She stood stock still, staring.

"Don't faint, please, Annabel. It's me, Robert."

"You could have warned me," said Annabel.

"But if I had, I wouldn't have seen your face like that!"

"Tie your horse to that tree and come in. I'll call Ben and Bo."

"Not yet. Let's talk a little first."

"It's so nice to see you again."

"The fresh air really has brought the color to your face, Ann," he said, smiling.

"You wouldn't believe how good I feel these days, Rob."

They went inside and sat in the front room.

"Now, I want to tell you that the drawings you sent are very good. I brought them back with me. I want to talk to Ben about a correspondence course. I must have your permission first, however. I would pay for the cost and send him materials. The agreement would be that at the end of it, he would allow me to be his agent and handle his artwork to sell."

Annabel took a quick breath. "Do you really like them? I mean, are they really that good?"

"Yes, indeed."

"I'm a little surprised. I thought his work good but I certainly didn't think that far."

"With a few lessons, I expect him to be even better." He stood up. "Now, show me around your lovely spot in the mountains."

Ben, Bo and Robert sat at the table drinking coffee, while Annabel cut another piece of apple pie. Finally, Annabel said, "Ben, Mr. Ingress wants to talk to you about your art work."

Ben looked up from his plate. "My art work? Oh, you mean my drawings?" He looked at their guest with more interest. "Is he your friend that you sent them to in Atlanta?"

"Yes," answered Annabel. "He likes them and wants to talk to you about them."

"Sit down and enjoy your pie, Ann, and we will talk about the art later."

Ben finished his dessert, but kept stealing glances at the stranger.

In the parlor, Robert opened his briefcase, took out Ben's drawings, and returned them to Annabel.

Addressing Ben as though he were a grown man, he said, "I'm very impressed with your work, Ben. I think you have real talent. I would like to make an offer, with your mother's approval, of course. I would like to sponsor you in an art course through the mail. I would send you all your paints and materials, and pay your tuition. I have already discussed this with your mother."

Ben gulped. "Why would you want to do that?"

"I want to be your agent. I would have the sole right to sell your artwork, and I would accept a small percent of the profits. You would sign a contract to this effect, and your mother and brother would be witnesses. What do you think?"

Ben gulped again, then shyly asked, "Do you actually think I'm that good?"

"I think you will become a very accomplished artist once you complete the correspondence course."

"Does that mean through the mail? We don't get mail delivered up here." Ben looked downcast.

"We can go through the Post Office in Norma. I've been doing that to write to your mother."

"What do you think, Mama?" Ben looked up eagerly.

Annabel smiled. "This is what I've been hoping for, Son. I think it's an excellent idea. Would you like to try it?"

"Oh, yes, Mama. Thank you Mr. Ingress!" Ben was beaming.

"Then we can sign the papers now." Robert reached again for his briefcase.

After a few more minutes, Robert said "I need to get back down the mountain and get this horse back to the boarding house. I leave in the morning." Annabel walked out with him to say goodbye and waved as he rode off down the trail.

Bo said, "Well, *Mister Tarwater*, if you can spare a few minutes, we have pigs to feed."

The three of them had a good laugh as they went about the evening chores.

George Wilson

George Wilson was on the porch with his father. "Papa, I want to talk to you about my future. I've been saving my money, and I want to go to Kingsport to be with Dent. I want to go to school and learn to be a surveyor."

Will frowned just a little. "Well, that's an ambitious plan, Son. It will cost a lot of money. I can help some, but I doubt I could pay the whole tuition."

"I've saved up every penny I could, and I would be staying at Dent and Dee's house. I would be working in the furniture store on weekends and whenever else I could."

"Does Dent know about this?"

"I'll go get his letters." George went to his bedroom and brought out a shoebox from under his bed. Inside were Dent's letters and several bills.

Turning to his father, George said, "here's the money I've already saved. Read Dent's letters and you will see that he wants me to come."

Will was impressed. "I had no idea that you had this much money." He pulled out the top envelope, opened it, and began reading:

Dear George,

I'm glad to get your letter. You've done well and I'm proud of you. Come and stay in our guest room and we'll talk over your options. Dee would like to have you, too.

Will looked up from the letter. "While I read the rest of these, go see if Silas has any work you can do for the next hour. I'll have to discuss this with your mother."

During the next two days, George wrote to Dent, packed clothes, and prepared to leave. Lydia wrote a letter for him to deliver to his brother and sister-in-law in Kingsport.

John followed his big brother around the entire time, finally confessing, "I don't want you to go, George."

George appeased him by promising, "I'll write you all the time." Then he scowled, "You stay out of trouble, now, you hear me? Or I'll come back and ... !"

John punched George lightly on the shoulder, then walked quickly away.

****

Silas picked up the mail in town and asked Andrew, "How does Dora like the job at the new neighbor's house?"

"Very much, indeed. Mrs. Stone has had her organ shipped here, and she's teaching Dora to play. Dora's teaching Becky to make biscuits, so they're both enjoying the arrangement."

"That's good to hear."

Silas dropped off the envelopes for the Wilsons on his way home. There were letters from Martha, Dent and George. Will sat down and read Martha's first.

Dearest Papa,

It seems ages since I first arrived here. At first I helped Dee a lot. Then I looked for work. I've found a good position in a dress shop. The owner has offered me a room here so I don't have to travel so much. She's a fascinating woman and designs lady's clothes. I'm so happy here, but I miss you so much. I keep the kitchen and shop for her once per week. I'm enjoying my walks to the market and butcher. Whatever I purchase is delivered later. Isn't that nice? I can walk home and enjoy the flowers and things.

I will come home and visit when I can, but it will be a while.

Your loving daughter, Martha.

Dent had written:

Dear Papa.

We are happy to report that George is doing well here and we are delighted to have him. It's a promising career and my father-in-law is very pleased with him. He tells me George is bright and determined to study hard and is also is doing well in the store. He is willing to sweep up, greet customers or anything that is asked of him. Dee says she is very happy to have him here. He already has won over our Lonny, who adores him. He will be writing soon to tell you more.

Love to Mama and the others.

Your obedient son, Dent.

The third letter was a short note from George. He told of his arrival and his visit to a school to discuss his plans. He promised to write more at a later time.

Caroline's Summer Break

Caroline had come home, but just for the summer break. She planned to return to school in Knoxville in September. She was glad to be on the farm again and was eager to get out in the open once more. She took the children swimming and visited the Lawson family and Mrs. Creech, who had not been well of late.

She put on old clothes and boots and announced she wanted to pick peas in the field.

Will said, "You don't have to do that just yet, Caroline. Relax a bit first."

"No, Papa. I've been inside all day for months, either in class or studying in my room; now I want to get out in the garden like the old days and help out."

She found her old straw hat and when she tied the ribbon under her chin, her younger sister teased her, saying, "You look comical."

The whole family laughed, and Caroline joined in. "I guess I feel sort of comical too, Nancy."

Her little brother Michael added, "You don't look like a city girl now."

"Go ahead and laugh, but it's good to be back here in the country, anyway."

There was a special bond between Will and Caroline and he loved having his middle daughter home.

Silas was picking peas in the field. When he saw her and Will coming he called to them. "Get a basket and start over there by the fencerow."

Caroline was busy with her thoughts in the warm sunshine, enjoying the lovely day. Will picked peas a few feet away. He was startled by her scream. He dropped his basket and leapt across the leafy vines to her side.

"A snake! A snake there, Papa! It got me."

A long, stout, dark gray snake was disappearing under the pea vines. Will grabbed Caroline as she began to slide to the ground. He pulled out his pocket knife and quickly carved an "x" across the two puncture wounds in the tender flesh on the inner part of her elbow. She screamed again but he ignored her, concentrating on sucking out the venom and spitting it onto the ground. "Quick, Silas. Go for the doctor."

Silas was already on his way, running as fast as he could to get a horse from the pasture.

Will kept sucking the venom out of the wound, until finally he picked up his daughter and rushed toward the house.

Silas saw Jasmine running from their cabin beyond the barn, and yelled to her, "Snakebite! Caro!" and kept running. He vaulted over the fence rail, grabbed the closest mare, jumped onto her back, and galloped bareback down the road to Norma.

Dr. McDonald came as fast as his horses could go to the Wilson home. He grabbed his black bag and hurried to the porch. "What kind?"

"Rattler. A big one. Help her, Doc." Will's hands were trembling, and he suddenly sat on the porch step, hard, as his knees buckled.

The doctor wrapped a tourniquet around Caroline's upper arm, drew more blood from the wound, then carried her inside and placed her on the sofa.

Caroline awoke and stared at her father and the doctor.

"The doc's here, honey. Lie still." Will patted her shoulder, feeling helpless.

Lydia stood in the middle of the room, so stunned she couldn't speak.

Silas and Jasmine stood silently by, grasping each other's hands.

"Did you rinse your mouth, Will?" asked the doctor

"No, I didn't think." Will went to the kitchen and rinsed his mouth with water from the pump.

Nancy and Michael both started crying loudly. Lydia tugged them back out of the room, praying as she went, "Don't take her, Lord. Don't take my baby. Be quiet, Nancy. You too, Michael. Mama needs you to be good right now. Oh, Lord please don't take Caro away from us. Please don't take my baby, please!"

Jasmine with Little Si in her arms said gently, "I'll stay with the kids, Lydia. You go back to Will."

Caroline's face was white, while the doctor sat in a chair beside her turning the tourniquet to keep it tight. "We have to keep her quiet, Will."

Lydia stared at a towel that lay on the floor, soaked with Caroline's blood.

Hours later John came quietly into the room. He had ridden from Norma as soon as he heard. He stayed with his parents, silently praying.

By sunset, the waiting was over. The doctor pulled the sheet over Caroline's face, and Lydia collapsed. John and the doctor caught her as she fell.

Will had gone outside, standing alone in the gathering dusk. Bats circled overhead and frogs croaked in the pond. But Will was deaf to the sounds. He was numb with grief.

John came out, saying gently, "Come back in, Papa."

Will only shook his head. He walked over and sat down on a bale of hay and bowed his head on his arms.

"Why Lord? How could You let this happen? Why? My little Caroline? Why couldn't I save her?"

Darkness settled over the barn. Shadows turned to blackness. John went into the house, then came back and lit a lantern and hung it on a nail.

"Papa," he said, "Papa, Mama is worried. Won't you come in and sit with her a while?"

"I'm no good to her right now, son. I failed her. I failed my little girl. Leave me. I want to be alone."

John met Silas as he was returning to the house. "He blames himself. He wants to be alone. He sent me away."

Doc gave Lydia a sedative. "Send for her other children, Silas. She'll need them all now. Do what you can."

Jasmine prepared Caroline for the wake. Looking through her clothes chest, she found a soft blue dress with a white lace collar, and dressed her in it. Caroline's face was white and distorted, but she was clean and beautiful.

Earl made a coffin for her in his shop, using his finest woods. Caroline lay in the parlor with flowers surrounding her. Neighbors and friends came to console the family, and helped them however they could, taking care of the animals and bringing pot luck dishes to share.

Doctor McDonald conferred with Pastor Greene, speaking quietly.

"Amos, Caroline must be buried tomorrow."

"But Dent and the others won't have time to get here."

"I know, but it's necessary to have the funeral as quickly as possible."

"I'll talk to Will. He's crushed. I don't know if I can get through to him, but I'll try."

Amos Greene found Will exhausted with grief. He hadn't been eating and had had very little sleep. The Pastor laid a hand on his shoulder.

"I need to talk to you, Will. My heart goes out to you. I wish I could help." He paused, then continued, "we need to talk about the funeral."

"Whatever you want, Pastor. The church, the cemetery. Will you take care of everything for me?"

"Of course. We'll carry her to the church tomorrow."

"So soon? But I'm not ready to let her go!"

"We must, Will. It can't be helped."

"I must talk to Lydia." Will rubbed his forehead, pulling his hands across his eyes. "I tried to save her, Pastor. I don't know what else I could have done to save her."

"You did your best. Don't blame yourself. For Lydia's sake, try to hold up."

Lydia fell into Will's arms when she saw him enter the room, and their tears merged in the misery that overtook them. Nothing was said for a long while. Will held her, and then laid her down on the sofa.

"Lydia, Pastor Greene and I have decided to have the funeral tomorrow."

"But, Will. The children ..."

"Word has already been sent to Martha, George and Dent. They'll be here as soon as they can. Meanwhile, let's try to eat something and try to hold up for the children's sake."

He helped Lydia stand up, and with his arm around her, led her to the laden table. Jasmine brought them coffee, and they forced themselves to swallow some food. Nancy came and leaned against her father's knee.

He embraced her and said, "My little Nancy. Did you eat, my dear?"

"Yes Papa," she replied. "Jasmine said I must. Papa, Jasmine said Martha and Dent will come?"

"Yes, and George too, but it will be days before they can travel all the way here. You must be a good girl, and be patient. We need you to help take care of Michael."

"I'm always good, Papa." She raised her little chin and tried hard to look strong and grown up.

Will bowed his head and prayed to God that He would help them get through another day.

Their friends, dressed in their Sunday best, gathered at the little white church in Norma and after a few heartfelt words from Pastor Greene, all said goodbye to the lovely Caroline. She was laid to rest in the churchyard under many floral offerings.

Lydia was helped to the buggy by Will and John. She had swollen eyelids and burning eyes from all the bitter tears she had cried. Her friends and neighbors, with their hearts aching too, were helpless to console her.

Kathy and Stella broke down at their friend's flower-covered graveside and were supported by their husbands.

Eli Greene, the pastor's son, stood quietly to one side during the entire afternoon, dealing with his own dashed dreams and broken heart.

"Such a sad time," said Evie to Earl. "It will take them forever to get over this."

Friends came back to the Wilson home and sat quietly sharing memories of the beautiful and talented middle daughter of Will and Lydia.

Dr. McDonald gave Lydia something to make her sleep, but once again Will refused to take anything.

"I'll sleep soon enough," he said. "I can't hold out much longer anyway. Your bill will be paid, Doctor."

"I know, Will. I know. Forget it now, and get some rest."

Martha, Dent and George returned and joined the family in their home in Norma. Jasmine took care of the meals so they could visit, and weep, together.

The brothers placed more flowers on the grave. Then they transplanted a rose bush to a sunny spot by the fence. It would soon grow and climb the fence post; its scarlet blooms would be a remembrance of Caroline for years to come. They walked away in silence.

Charlie and Thelma and Rueben

Charlie and Rube sat at the table, while Thelma put Matthew to bed. Rube held a pad and pencil.

"The money from the sale of Thelma's farm won't last long. We need to figure out what we need to get us through the coming winter and to work out a budget for our expenses."

Thelma came and sat with them. "I want the money to go for repairs on the house. This is our home."

Charlie agreed, but added, "we'll have other expenses besides the house. We'll need to buy seeds and a cow and maybe a hog, as well as pay our taxes. I've been thinking, we should put our accounts together and have only one service charge from the bank. We can add to it as we go along with selling herbs and things. I'll be going back to Huntsville to work in the brick factory in May, or maybe even sooner, whenever warm weather returns. Until then, we need to make a budget. We need to think about what seeds we should buy for the coming garden, and what it will take to get us through. Since we don't have canned goods yet, like we will next year, we'll have to hunt and fish and such to make do."

Rube said, "we must think of getting the house ready for cold weather, too. I need to get wood to chop for the fires. That's important right now."

****

Earl had a letter from Charlie and he shared the information with Evie. "Charlie's off work at the brickyard until spring. Meanwhile, he's bought a cow, and wants me to make him a churn and dashers."

"I already have one made up in the shop," Earl continued. "Tomorrow, I should take it down there; that'll give me an excuse to go see Charlie."

"That's a good idea," agreed Evie.

He stored the new churn in the wagon along with baskets of grapes, apples and pears. Evie brought out several jars of peaches and string beans.

"They'll need these," she commented, handing the small containers to Earl. "They didn't have time to get much of a garden in at Rube's place."

The next morning, he set off for New River. He stopped at the store to get his mail, told Stella that he would be gone overnight, and asked if she or Carrie would spend the day and night with Evie. Stella said, "one of us will, Earl. Here, take some of this fresh butter and bread for them to have until they can make their own."

"Tell them hello for us," added Andrew.

****

At the end of a long tiring day, Earl reached the Miller house with aching arms, and cramped legs. The rutted road had been especially rough this trip.

Charlie was surprised to see Earl drive his team into the yard. He hurried to help him unhitch the horses. "I'll feed them some oats and rub them down after we get you into the house," said Charlie. "Then we can let them run loose in the field. There's water out there."

Gladly Earl let Charlie walk him to the door.

"Look who's here, Thelma!"

After Thelma served her most welcome guest supper, she put the baby to bed and returned to the living room.

Earl said, "Evie and the Harness's send you their love. I have fruit and things in the wagon that need to be taken out before morning, Charlie. Will you go with me to get them?"

When they had taken in the things, including the new churn, Earl said to Charlie, "now that you're off work until May, I was wondering if you could come out to The Clearing and work for me again? We always worked so well together. I need to make some improvements on the house, and I have orders I need to work on in the shop as well."

"Thank you Earl. I'd like that. But I couldn't be gone all week. Did we tell you Thelma is expecting another baby? Let's go talk to her. Can you take the other side of this basket?"

When they all had discussed the offer, there was a general agreement that two days of working each week, with two traveling days, would work well for everyone until the brickyard opened in May. The extra income would help a lot with repairs on the Rube's house, and the extra help would be good for Earl at the shop.

Charlie said he would start immediately.

While Charlie was gone, Rube put shelves in the cellar, made a plank floor, and set Thelma's crock there that she would use for making kraut. He made a bin for potatoes and pumpkins and hung pegs for dried beans and onions, herbs and household tools. Charlie was very pleased when he returned and saw all the improvements.

"Thelma, here's a jar of honey that Lydia Wilson sent," said Charlie. Matthew wanted to be held and he obliged, asking, "did you miss me, little man?"

When he left again for Norma the air was cold, but Charlie was dressed warmly with long knitted underwear under his overalls and a warm coat and gloves. He urged the plodding horse onward as fast as the rough road permitted, for the sky was overcast, and he worried about snow falling before he reached Earl's house. He wondered if he could keep his bargain of traveling to Norma every week once the weather turned bad.

Ben Tarwater

Ben Tarwater rode into Norma to the general store regularly for supplies and the mail. He posted his assignments to Atlanta and picked up his art supplies and letters for his mother. Andrew had told Ezra about Ben, describing him as a budding artist, and Ezra was anxious to meet him and see his drawings.

One cold rainy day, Ben was on his way to the store with a package to mail. He had it protected beneath his oil slicker. When he passed Ezra's house, the artist called to him to wait up, and come in and wait for the rain to stop. He invited Ben into his studio where his stove had heated up the rooms. He had a coffee pot atop the stove.

"I keep things out here, so I don't have to stop and go to the house, interrupting my work," Ezra explained. He offered Ben a cup of coffee and a piece of cake from the tin on the shelf. They discussed Ben's work and his progress. Ezra showed him some of his own watercolors depicting the colorful mountains and scenery around Norma.

"I would like to see some of your art sometime, Ben."

"I would like to do that, sir. I'll stop here and bring a few paintings the next time I come for the mail."

When the rain slackened, Ben left Ezra's and took his mother's shopping list to Andrew at the store.

Andrew talked to him as he filled the order. "We would like you to attend church with us some Sunday, Ben, if you and your family would come. You wouldn't have to ride back right away; you could have dinner with us."

"I'll talk to Mama and Bo about it," answered Ben. "Thanks for asking." He dropped off his package at the Post Office counter and waved a cheery goodbye as he left the store with his mother's order.

****

October arrived and colder weather set in. Earl had finished the room addition and the porch on his house. There was a large pile of wood chopped and neatly stacked outside his kitchen door.

"I think I need to spend more time at home, Earl," said Charlie. "It's getting harder to travel, and it would be more dangerous if I should get caught in snow on the road."

"I agree," said Earl. "We're pretty well set here, and you need to prepare for winter there in New River. Rube probably needs your help more than I do."

"Then I'll plan on leaving soon."

"Thanks, Charlie, for all you've done. You're a good friend." He paid Charlie his wages and asked, "Will you be leaving tomorrow or Friday?"

"I may as well start early tomorrow, if the skies are clear. I'll say goodbye to Amy tonight. She may still be asleep when I leave."

"Then we'd better go tell my girls that you are going."

****

The next day, Charlie reached New River just before dark. He was surprised to see such a big change in the appearance of the house with the lamps throwing light from the windows. He called out to Thelma and Rube, saying he would bed down the horse and be right in.

"We didn't expect you until Friday," said Rube. "But I'm glad you're here. Reverend Wilcox and my brother brought some of the church members over one sunny day and worked on the house. They were afraid it wouldn't be finished before snow, so he asked in church if they would help us out. They are very good people."

"Bring a lamp," said Thelma, "and I'll show you the new rooms. They turned out so nice."

She started to lead him through the door, then stopped and turned.

"I'm so happy you're home for good."

"Me, too. I've missed you so much," he said as he gave her a long kiss.

Ben and Hallie

Ben and Ezra had become good friends.

Ezra had painted mountain scenes which had been very well received in Philadelphia. They were done in oils, and he showed them to Ben, introducing him to that medium so Ben could experience painting in a different way. He advised Ben on the assignments he was mailing to Atlanta.

They spent time in his studio and ate together at his house. Ben loved Dora's berry cobbler and her wild grape jelly. "I wish my mother could make this dessert," he said, cleaning up the last crumbs from his plate.

"Then just bring her on down, and we'll see that she learns how to do it," said Rose.

Ezra added, "By all means, ask her to visit. We would love to have her, and Rose would have someone to talk to about things she misses in Philadelphia. Big cities have so much in common."

"I believe she'd like that. I'll tell her."

One day when he arrived at the Stone's house, Dora's youngest sister, Hallie Lawson, was there visiting. He mentioned the differences in the sisters' hair and complexions. Hallie had lovely auburn hair and a slim figure and he thought her quite dainty.

"I take after my mother," she explained. "She died during a big storm a few years ago." She sighed, then continued, "Dora is more like Papa."

Changing the subject, she asked, "Did you say your mother was from Atlanta?"

"Yes. She went to college there before she was married. My father inherited the property on the mountain and that's why we're here in Tennessee."

When Ben said he had to go, Hallie walked him to the door.

Autumn in Scott County

With the first hard freeze, Will announced that it was time to kill the hogs. It was a busy time for everyone, but finally the rows of canned sausage in glass jars sat on the shelf behind the stove, and the hams and other cuts of pork were in the smokehouse. Lydia fried enormous amounts of chops for the table. After supper everyone sat resting before the fire eating popcorn and talking.

The next week, John built a fire under the iron pot in the back yard. Lydia, Hallie and Jasmine cut up pieces of fat pork into pans and dropped them into the pot to render them into lard. The lard was used for baking, frying and making cream gravy which all of them liked with their meals. While the women worked with the pork, Will and Silas brought firewood to the yard and kept the fire going.

Will slowly began feeling the burdens of sadness lifting from his heart.

When the frost cleared and the weather warmed up a bit, Annabel, Ben and Bo accepted an invitation to stay a few days with Rose and Ezra in Norma.

Rose was pleased to have guests, and thoroughly enjoyed talking with Annabel. She mentioned that her two sons, living back home in Philadelphia, would be coming to visit for Christmas. "I want you to come and meet them then."

"I would love to do that," Annabel replied.

Thanksgiving at New River

Charlie had gone hunting hoping for a turkey for their Thanksgiving dinner. The light snow had melted but a cold wind blew over the forest. He saw squirrels, but held his fire and waited patiently for a turkey to show himself in the brush. He had a turkey call that Rube had whittled and he used it to lure a male out of hiding. At last he gobbled and the huge bird appeared over a low bush. Charlie aimed accurately and it fell into the brush. Thelma would be so pleased. On the way back he killed two rabbits which he dressed out and put in the smoke house to await another day.

Charlie wrote a letter to his mother and sent it to the post office in Norma. He asked her if she and the boys wanted to spend the Thanksgiving weekend with him at Thelma and Rube's farm.

Annabel wrote back and told him she would like to come, but Ben and Bo had both been invited to the

Wilson home for the holiday, and they wanted to go there instead.

Charlie drove up to visit Earl and Evie, and Ben brought his mother down to Earl's house. After they had visited a bit and spent the night, Annabel left with Charlie for New River.

Rube was delighted to see Annabel again. He told her about the new rooms, the cellar and the new chimney.

Charlie listened smiling; for he was glad they were such good friends.

Annabel wanted to see the improvements to the house, even though she was very tired from the long trip down to New River. But Thelma said, "Annabel, I'll get you settled first. We have days to talk. You must be ready to drop."

****

Meanwhile, at The Wilson's house in Norma, there was much excitement. Cooking had been going on for three days. The turkey was baking and pies and cookies were baking. There would be no lack of all the extras that the Wilson family expected every Thanksgiving.

Good smells came from the kitchen, and the roaring fire on the hearth was keeping everyone warm while they chatted and waited for Lydia to call them in to eat turkey with all the trimmings.

****

Charlie and Thelma were enjoying hosting Thanksgiving dinner at New River. The house was cozily warm, and Matthew had eaten, and been put down for his nap.

The four adults were still sitting at the table, too satisfied to move. "You're an excellent cook, Thelma."

"Thank you. I'm happy you're here. I've missed you."

"And I'm proud of you, too, Charlie, for providing that nice fat turkey." Annabel smiled contentedly.

Rueben spoke up. "Let's take a walk, Annabel, we need some exercise." She got her shawl and went outside with him.

"Wouldn't it be wonderful if Papa and your mother became engaged, Charlie?"

"I wouldn't be a bit surprised," said Charlie. "I sort of hope they do."

Christmas in Scott County

Sam cut a tree to trim for Christmas and stood it in the corner. Carrie and James were excited to have a tree in their very first home with Sam. They spent some time getting to know all of Sam's step-daughters. Of course Kathy's husband Paul was with her, along with their son Sammy; Andrew came with Stella, and their twin boys were the center of attention.

The little white church was the focus of activity for the holiday. Families came to listen to Pastor Greene tell the Christmas Story. His wife arranged a children's program. Nancy and Amy were dressed as angels, and Michael was a wise man in the pageant. Sacks of hard candy and fruit were given to everyone at the end of the program, and it was all over in time for the folks to get back to their homes before dark.

At the Stone residence, Rose and Ezra were expecting their sons to arrive. Dora and Rose had been cooking and all was ready. Ezra finally said at one o'clock, "we'll eat now. We don't know when the boys will arrive. Rose, will you tell Dora to serve the turkey?"

Rose had really hoped that Thomas and Jeffrey would get there by Christmas Day. Becky tried to fill in for her brothers' presence, but she knew she couldn't fill their shoes in her mother's eyes. After a subdued supper, Rose went to bed very disappointed. Ezra did his best to console her, and she finally went to sleep.

The next morning a cold wind blew from the north. There were snow flurries and Ezra was concerned, but he managed not to show it to Rose and Becky. There were ample leftovers, including turkey and pies, for their meals.

Dora asked if she could go to Stella's across the street and visit with her sister and Andrew.

Ezra said "of course. Go ahead, Dora. If we need you we'll send for you."

It was nearing dark when the carriage finally arrived from the south, and stopped in the street. The two men looked at each other. "I'm sure this is the right place," Thomas finally spoke. "There's the store and here's the house. But you go on up and make sure, Jeff."

Jeffrey knocked and Ezra opened the door, yelling "The boys are here, Rose."

More quietly, he said, "Tie the horses to the rail, boys, then come on in. We'll take care of them shortly."

Rose rushed into Thomas' arms and Becky ran to Jeffrey.

"You came!" Becky said delightedly. "You made it! We have presents for you."

"Sorry we were delayed, Papa. The weather caught us and we had to wait until this morning."

"I'm just glad you're safe," said Ezra.

Rose couldn't stop smiling. She finally gathered her thoughts and said, "I'll just heat up some supper. Our girl, Dora, is out at the moment, but we have lots of leftovers, including turkey and pies."

"Good! I could use some hot coffee, too, Mother."

"Should I go for Dora, Rose?"

"I think not. In the morning will be soon enough. Their rooms are all ready."

"While the food is warming, Papa, show us where to take the horses."

They were retuning from the stable when Ezra saw Dora crossing the street. "Here's Dora now," he said to his sons.

"I saw the carriage, Mr. Stone," she said. "I came right away. Rose will need me, I'm sure."

"Dora, may I present my sons Jeffrey and Thomas?"

Both young men shook hands with the young maid.

"Brrr. Let's get inside out of this cold wind."

After the family had eaten, Rose said apologetically, "I hope you don't mind sharing a room; the house is quite small. Dora and Becky are sharing a room tonight, too."

"Of course we don't mind, Mother." The boys carried their bags to the room she indicated would be theirs.

When the brothers were alone, Thomas said. "I saw her first. Isn't she a beauty?"

"Keep your voice down, Tom. You don't know how thin these walls are."

"Just remember," Thomas said softly, "She's mine!"

Jeffrey said, "Fine, Brother. Do your best. If you don't win her, I get a chance."

When Ezra looked out the window the following morning, he saw snow covering the streets. It was beautiful, but he knew it meant additional work before they could enjoy it.

"Come, boys. Let's shovel out to the barn and feed the stock. Then we'll shovel to my studio and you can see where I work. I must get some sketches of this beautiful snowfall before it gets all tracked up and dirty."

Dora and Becky washed dishes and made the beds. "We must decide the dinner," said Rose. "What do we have on hand, Dora? Will we need to go to the store?"

As the women talked, Ezra was showing his studio to his sons with a great amount of pride.

Ezra invited a few neighbors in to dinner to meet his sons. Dora served and Rose charmed her guests, as an accomplished hostess. When a knock sounded at the door, Dora went to answer. It was Ben Tarwater, asking to speak to Ezra.

Dora spoke quietly. "Go see what he wants Ezra," she said. "I think he's too shy to talk to me."

"I'm sorry, Ezra, I didn't know you were having company. It can wait." Ben turned and went back outside, but Ezra followed him to the wagon.

"Ben, please. That doesn't matter. What did you want to speak to me about?"

"It's personal," he stammered. "I'll come back another day."

"We're friends, Ben. You know I'm here for whatever you need."

"Well, it's confidential, of course," began Ben.

"Of course. I understand."

"Well, it's Hallie. I really like her, but I've been living on the mountain so long I don't even know how to talk to a girl. How can I speak to her? She's at Will's house but I don't even have an excuse to go over there."

"You don't need a reason, Ben. Hallie is an intelligent girl. She probably feels the same as you. Just knock on the door, and tell Lydia that you'd like to speak to Hallie alone, if she isn't busy. Lydia will understand that you want privacy. Then simply ask her if you can see her home from church on Sunday."

"Yes, I guess I could do that." said Ben, slowly.

"Are you staying at Perkin's?"

"Yes, Mama's at Charlie's, and Bo and I are staying at the boarding house."

"When you come back from the Wilson's, come here and eat supper with us. Do you have lanterns on the wagon? Be careful on the slippery places." He added, "and good luck with Hallie!"

It had turned colder by the time Ben drove into the lane and tied up at the hitching rail. When he knocked on the door, he was surprised that Hallie answered. He wasn't prepared to talk to her just yet. He had expected to see Lydia first. He didn't know what to say, but she spoke first.

"Ben! How nice to see you. Come in."

"I can't stay, Hallie. I need to get back soon." He took a deep breath, then blurted out, "I just wanted to ask you if I could see you Sunday? I could bring you home from church if you like."

"I would like that very much." Hallie smiled happily. "You can stay for supper here tonight if you like. Lydia will be happy to see you."

"Thanks, but I'll be going now. I'll see you on Sunday."

Lydia walked by and saw him at the door just as he was turning away. "Ben, won't you stay for supper?"

"No, thanks, Mrs. Wilson. I must get back to the boarding house. It'll be dark soon."

Ben drove back to town in the borrowed wagon. He was too excited to join the crowd at Ezra's, so he just went straight to Perkin's to have supper with Bo.

Bo was waiting for him, "I wanted to make sure you got back safely," he said. "It may snow tonight and we may be stuck here for a while."

"Yes, I wanted to get in before it got worse outside." He took his packages to his bedroom and went to wash up.

"Let's go see what Mrs. Perkins has cooked up for us, Brother."

****

The next day was Sunday, and Ezra wanted to take his sons to the Baptist Church in Norma, so they could experience the country citizens at worship. They decided to take the wagon, and use the wagon bed. Thomas helped his mother and Dora up to the wagon seat and Ezra, Becky and Jeffrey climbed into the back. They merrily left for the short trip to the church.

Dora was wearing the new black cloak and bonnet that the Stones had given her for Christmas and Thomas looked her over, thinking how beautiful she was. Rose was not particularly pleased to notice his glances, although she thought that indeed Dora, flushed with cold, was truly very pretty.

Ezra was aware of Rose's tight-lipped appearance. He understood the reason, for he, too, had noticed Thomas' interest in the pretty hired girl. He was a little disappointed himself because he wanted Thomas to marry into his publisher's family. However, he also wanted his sons to be happy and make their own choices. He thought, "I'll hear about this tonight when Rose and I are beneath the blankets cozy and warm."

Because the weather was threatening, and because everyone had been to church just a couple of days earlier for the special service, Pastor Greene made the service quite brief, and sent his congregation home again after saying just a few words and leading them in one or two hymns.

"Hardly worth coming out for," commented Jeffrey, "but I suppose it was best to get everyone home quickly."

Once again Dora sat with Rose on the wagon seat. She chattered about leaving early tomorrow to go for a visit with the Redmonds.

"My brother-in-law, Paul, will come for me with a sled. I'm looking forward to seeing Kathy and little Sammy. I'll have time to make a cake when I get there, and then I'll be back in two days. Thanks for letting me have this time."

Rose graciously responded, "Since our meal is already prepared, and just needs reheating, and the desserts are waiting in the pantry, I'm sure I can do fine without you for the rest of the holiday."

As Ezra had expected, Rose expressed her thoughts to him just as soon as the two of them were in bed that night.

"Really! I hadn't expected Thomas to act like a seventeen year old chatting up Dora like that. He'll soon be going back to Philadelphia, and Dora will be hurt. How can he be so insensitive?"

"Now, Rose, he and Agatha aren't exactly engaged to be married, you know. He probably isn't serious about Dora."

"If he's going to act childishly, I'm going to be very disappointed in him. Dora is not the type to be a businessman's wife. How could she be expected to run his house in a city like Philadelphia?" Rose was quite indignant.

"You're probably right. I, myself, was rather hoping Thomas would be happy with the daughter of my friend, Clayton. However, we can't make these decisions for our children. So let's not cross any bridges, my dear. Let's just get some sleep. Things will settle down, I hope."

Rose sniffed, "At least she'll be away for two days and Jeffrey and Thomas will be leaving as soon as the roads are passable. They have to be back at school by January second."

After a short pause, she added, "But you're right, Ezra. I am a little tired. Perhaps we'd better go to sleep."

The next day Ezra showed his sons around town and proudly introduced them to more of his friends. Rose was equally proud of them. Time passed most pleasantly, but to Rose's dismay, Dora returned slightly earlier than she had hoped.

While Jeffrey kept their parents occupied, Thomas asked Dora to walk with him to the stable to take care of his horses.

"I want to get to know you better, Dora."

"We have only just met, Thomas."

"I know, but I won't be here long, and I want to make every minute count."

She stood by while he fed the horses, and noticed that he spoke to each one like a treasured pet. Then he turned to Dora, looked into her eyes, and pulled out a box from his coat pocket.

"I got this for Mother." He explained. "But she has plenty of jewelry, and I have already given her a present. I want you to have this."

She opened the box. It contained a beautiful necklace.

"Oh, Thomas, I can't take this expensive jewelry."

"Yes, you can. I want you to wear it and think of me. And I want you to write to me. I will write you every day, and you must answer. How do you get your mail?"

Dora explained about the Post Office in the general store, and he said, "I'll remember. Promise me you'll answer."

He took her hand and kissed it.

"Yes, I will, Thomas, and thank you. Please don't mention the necklace to anyone. I don't want to have to explain it."

"I understand, Dora. It's our secret. Let's go back now. Mother is very smart. We mustn't be gone too long."

It was much warmer when Thomas and Jeffrey set out to return to Philadelphia. Everyone gathered in the yard to say goodbye, except Dora. She watched from a bedroom window, her fingers holding the necklace under her blouse.

Ezra warned his sons. "Don't try to make up time, boys. Don't take any chances."

"Don't worry, Father. We aren't in any hurry to get back to classes. We'll be careful. Would you bring that good warm rug for our feet?" Jeffrey asked, adding,

"And please hand me that basket of goodies you packed for us, Mother."

Thomas spoke up. "Here's our little sister to give us a hug. Goodbye, little one."

The brothers embraced their mother, then kissed Rebecca.

"Next year Papa will have had his year in the mountains, Becky, and you'll be back in dear old Philadelphia."

Thomas said, "You will write us often, won't you?"

"I promise. I will. Oh. I told Mama I wouldn't cry."

"Of course you won't cry. There's a good girl. We'll send you postcards from every stop we make."

Cheerfully, the two young men drove down the road toward New River, while Ezra called, "take care," and hurried Rose inside out of the chill.

Dora watched from the window still holding the necklace tightly. "I mustn't cry," she thought. "I must not let Rose or Ezra see me weeping." She continued to watch until the carriage rolled away out of sight, thinking, "if Rose knew about this, I would not be working in her house another day." Then she smiled. "After all, Thomas is a very handsome man and has lots of money." She hurried to the kitchen and began to wash pots and pans.

Ezra and his wife went inside. He could tell that Rose was very sad. "I'll be glad when spring arrives and we can go home," she said. She did not go into the kitchen, but sat in the parlor and stared into the blazing fire.

Ezra went through the house to the back door.

"I'll be in my shop, Dora," he said.

He continued to the shop and built a fire in the stove. He was behind schedule with his writing to send back to his publisher. "I'll catch up," he thought, "now that the boys are on their way back to school." There was a poem running through his mind and he hurried to get pen and paper.

"That's it!" he said aloud, "Back to work. That's the answer."

Wintertime

In Norma, and all across Scott County, the overnight snow was having its effect on the citizens.

At Reuben Miller's place, Charlie Tarwater's mother rose early, dressed warmly, and went to the kitchen to build up the fire in the cook stove. Usually Thelma was up by now. "She must not be feeling well," thought Annabel. She filled the coffeepot and teakettle with water and set them on the stove. She heard a sound in the next room and looked up as Charlie came into the kitchen.

"Is Thelma having morning sickness again?"

"Yes, I'm afraid so."

"Poor dear. I'll make her some tea as soon as I get the biscuits in the oven."

"That would be great, Mama. She really isn't up to cooking breakfast this morning. If I help, can you fix us something?"

"I certainly can, Son. I know where everything is though, so you won't have to do anything. Oh, you could take care of Matthew. That will help Thelma the most."

When breakfast was almost ready, Reuben came into the kitchen, followed closely by Charlie, carrying Matthew. He was talking softly to the little boy, crooning: "Be good, Son. Your mama isn't feeling well this morning."

Rueben looked out the kitchen window. "It snowed another inch last night," he said. "I'll dig a path to the barn after I eat breakfast."

Just then Thelma came in looking very pale. "It's so good of you, Annabel, to do this."

"I don't mind at all. Are you feeling any better?"

"Yes, some. Thanks for the tea. It helped a lot."

"Sit down and see if you can eat something now."

Matthew drank his milk and then asked, "Can I go out in the snow, Mama?"

Charlie touched Thelma on the arm. "Yes, do let him go. I'll take him out for a while after we get the snow shoveled." He bent down to kiss Thelma's pale cheek.

****

Meanwhile, at Sam Lawson's house, Kathy and Paul Redmond were talking to her younger sister Malinda.

The snow was making it hard to get to the outhouses, and Paul said, "I need one more cup of coffee; then I'll start to shovel."

Kathy pulled herself up from the table. "Honestly, I wish this baby would hurry and get here. I'm so tired of this clumsiness."

Malinda said, "I hope you have a girl this time."

"Me, too. I'd like to sew some girl dresses for a change."

"Well, don't get in too big a hurry. The doctor would find it hard to get here in this weather."

Paul poured more coffee. "I need to get busy. I miss Sam more than ever now on days like this."

"I miss Papa too, Paul. But have you noticed he has been much better since he married Amelia? I think he was lonelier than we ever thought."

"His health has certainly improved," answered Paul, on his way out the back door. "I better get that path cleared."

****

The snow melted as fast as it had arrived. Bo and Ben packed the wagon that Rueben had lent them and started down from Brimstone Mountain, headed for New River to see their mother and brother and his family. The road was muddy and they had to watch carefully.

Thelma greeted them warmly, and said, "It's so good to see you both again. I'll show you your rooms. Do you want to share or be separate?"

Ben spoke up first. "Let's be separate. I want to be alone some to paint on my new project, Thelma, if it's no trouble."

"I'll show you what we have and you may choose."

Ben chose a bedroom with morning light. He set up his easel and unpacked his clothes. He was eager to work on his painting.

Amelia Lawson

Amelia was sitting with her feet up and fanning herself vigorously. "Honestly, I wish this baby would hurry and get here. These days are so hot and miserable."

Carrie had finished the dishes and sat with her.

"I don't envy you in the least, Mama. A new baby after all these years. Sam is so proud, I wonder how he can stand it," she laughed.

"I want this baby too, Carrie. Since you and James are grown it'll be nice to have a little one in the house."

"In that case, I'm glad for you."

"I'm glad to have you helping me. The laundry and cooking are more than I could manage."

"Speaking of cooking, I'd better start on supper."

That night, everyone in Sam and Amelia's house was sleeping soundly. The night was quiet except for owls hooting in the forest. Sam was awakened by his wife, who was stirring in her sleep and groaning. He gently touched her arm.

"Are you all right? Were you dreaming?"

Amelia sat up suddenly, letting out a loud shriek.

"The baby, Sam! I'm having pains and it's too soon."

Sam hurried to light a lamp and called for Carrie and James.

"It's easing now, Sam," Amelia said. "Sorry for the bother. Maybe it was something I ate."

After everyone else had gone back to bed, Amelia continued to sit up for a while, propped up on her pillows.

Sam lay still, but stared into space. He was worried. "Tomorrow, I'll send for the doctor and he'll make sure. I want to be told that everything is all right," he thought.

Dawn approached gray and raining. Sam was up as soon as the first rooster crowed. He called for James.

"Go to Dr. McDonald's, and ask if he can come out to check your mother. I'll stay here in case she needs anything. Ride as fast as you can, but be careful."

Carrie was in the kitchen preparing breakfast and talking quietly to Sam when Amelia came in looking pale, wrapped in an old robe. She rushed to help her mother get seated at the table. "Mama, I'll get you ready for the doctor's visit. I'll change your bed and straighten the bedroom before he gets here. But let's eat now, and not waste any time."

Dr. McDonald was with Amelia for what seemed to be a very long time. Carrie went outside to walk because she was too nervous to sit still and wait for news. When the doctor finally came out of the bedroom, he asked Sam to go outside with him.

"Sam, you must remember Amelia's age. She's not as strong as I'd like her to be. I want her on complete bed rest. Try to get her to eat as much as she can and drink plenty of milk. I'll come out as often as I can. But she must stay in bed. Is that clear?"

"Yes, indeed, Doctor. I'll see to it. I'll send for my daughter to come help, because the house will be too much for Carrie to handle by herself. I'm sure Dora will be glad to help us out."

Bo Tarwater

Bo Tarwater was sick of hearing how wonderful his brother was and how successful he was becoming. He had been so close to Ben all these years, and Ben had looked out for him on so many occasions. Now Ben had no time for him. He was either in the studio painting or out some place sketching a mountain scene to paint. On Sundays he was with Hallie, while Bo had no one.

Bo had made up his mind. Instead of indulging in self-pity, he would save up as much cash as he could and go away; maybe to Carey, or even Knoxville. He could find work; there was no doubt in his mind about that. He would leave a letter for his mother and ride off early one morning. He could spend the first night at his older brother's house in New River. Then he would proceed on the next day. Charlie would welcome him for one night at least.

Annabel was sewing a new baby gown for Stella's baby, and stopped to talk to Ben and Bo.

"I'm getting restless." she told them. "I think I'll write to Charlie and Thelma. Perhaps they could use some help getting ready for winter."

Ben looked up from his plate.

"That may be a good idea, Mama. When do you plan this trip?"

"I'll wait for Charlie's answer," said Annabel.

"I may want to go down there too for a few days, said Ben. "They have some very nice hardwoods that will turn color soon. I can paint while I'm there."

Bo stood up abruptly, saying, "I'll just go attend to the horses."

In the stable he fumed to himself. Not once had either of the others asked him if he wanted to join them, or if he would be all right on the place alone or even what his wishes were. He determined to leave before winter.

Plans

Dora was finishing up hanging the laundry on the clothesline, while Carrie was in the kitchen churning. Sam sat with Amelia, fanning her with a cardboard fan. A slight breeze rustled the curtains near her bed.

Suddenly they heard Dora yelp. Sam rushed outside and saw the problem: she had stepped on a yellow jacket nest.

"Go quickly, and get some baking soda. Make a paste and put it on the stings. I'll take care of the nest."

Soon he was pouring kerosene into the open hole beneath the big old oak tree.

Dora, packing the gooey paste on her legs and ankles, trying to get relief from the pain of the yellow jacket stings, was not in a very good mood.

"Carrie, take care of supper. I'm going to my room." She stomped out of the kitchen. Carrie stared after her, but said nothing.

Sam came in and set the fuel can on a high shelf. "Yellow jackets are building early. It means a bad winter coming."

Dora heard him from her room. "I'm thinking of the winter too," she thought. "I'm the one who has to work every time one of my sisters gets pregnant; and now I'm working again with my step-mother."

The pain from the stings was subsiding now but she remained sitting on her bed. "I need new clothes and I need money; more than I have now. I need to make plans. Just as soon as Amelia's child arrives, I'll be ready."

****

Bo was working on his plans, too. He spent Saturdays in the mountains with tow-sacks and a game bag. He gathered herbs and wild grapes. He always carried his gun and fishing pole. He caught a nice string of the popular buffalo fish.

The innkeeper was glad to pay Bo for the fish and the grapes. The herbs he sold to Andrew Harness. Finally, late one night he sewed the money he had saved into his trousers for safekeeping, bathed, packed his saddlebags, and went to bed tired but satisfied.

The young man was on his way before dawn, having left a letter on his bed for his mother. He was happy, and felt free and light-hearted as he rode along.

Charlie and Rueben were surprised to see Bo ride up to their door. Thelma cooked one of his favorite foods, but as they sat and talked, Bo started to nod.

Thelma said, "Charlie, your brother's tired. Take him to his room and let him sleep."

****

On Sunday, Dora rode over to Anabell's. "I need a favor from you. It's confidential."

Anabell assured her young friend that her secret would be safe, whatever it might be.

"I want to borrow some money. I need so many things and I want to leave Norma as soon as Amelia delivers her baby."

"Where will you go?"

"I want to go to my friend Kirby Lee in Roane County. He worked here for the Wilsons years ago. I'm sure he and his wife Molly will help me find work there. I plan to study etiquette so I can be prepared if and when ... well, if I should ever have a chance to live in a grand home in Philadelphia."

Annabel was thrilled to hear of Dora's plans. She had been reared in Atlanta, and knew what it was to live in a big city and to be a lady.

"I'll be happy to help you, Dora. I must tell you that Bo also decided to leave Norma, and has already slipped off in the night. I hope you won't do such a thing. Please allow your friends to help you and share in your happiness. You can take your time paying me back. I wish you great success."

****

Annabel and her second son closed the house on the mountain and left for New River just as brilliant colors began appearing all over the country side. Annabel loved the red and orange foliage and Ben was itching to paint the lovely scenes as soon as he arrived at his brother's house. Thelma had their rooms ready and little Matthew and the new baby girl were noisily welcoming the company. Rueben came out and helped Ben take care of the team and prepare the horses for the night.

"I can't tell you how happy we are to see you both, Ben." Reuben turned a couple of large buckets upside down and let himself down to sit on one of them. "Here, sit with me a bit. I want to talk with you."

Ben joined him, sitting on the other pail. He was curious, but waited patiently to see what the older man would have to say.

"You know, Charlie and Thelma and the kids have their own lives, and I get to feeling like I'm in the way sometimes."

"Nonsense, Rueben. You make your way around here; and you know they love you."

"I know that. But I keep thinking I'm getting older and I want my own home." He took a breath. "And I want it with Annabel. Does that shock you?"

"Not at all, Reuben. I'm sure mother feels the same way. She's been restless for weeks wanting to be with you. I'm not in the least shocked. In fact, I was thinking of asking Hallie to marry me at Christmas, and I'll feel even better about that if I know you'll be with Mama."

"It would make me very happy to marry your mother," replied Rueben.

"It would seem we are in agreement. But let's talk more about it later. I'm ready to pull off these boots and get some rest."

Early the next morning Ben took his easel and paints and left for the woods. The colors were stunning and the streams made a good setting. He spent hours out there enjoying every minute. He was surprised to see his mother walking toward him as he was packing up his paints and brushes.

"Isn't it gorgeous in the woods?" asked Annabel. "I never tire of the mountains."

Ben agreed. "There is always something to paint, and the smells are just breath-taking. I love the chill in the air, too."

"Ben, let's sit for a minute." said Annabel. "I want to discuss something with you."

"Sure, sit here on my stool, Mama, and I'll sit on the ground."

"Ben, I know you're pictures are doing quite well in Atlanta. I've had letters from Rob, and he has enormous plans for you."

"Yes, Mama." Ben squinted against the sun as he looked up into Annabel's face.

"Well, Ben, I have an idea, and I've discussed it with Rueben. He has his eye on some property west of here that will be coming up for sale soon. He and Charlie have already bought some acreage from this neighbor, and now the fellow is selling out all his land and moving to his son's house. I was wondering if you might want to buy out our house? I could use some of the money to add to Rueben's to buy this land next to Charlie. Give it some thought. Don't decide right away."

Annabel paused, took a deep breath, and added, "And, oh yes, Rueben has asked me to marry him!"

Ben jumped to his feet and threw his arms around his mother.

"That's great news, Mama," he said. "And a great idea about the land and your house. Let's hurry back and talk to the others."

****

Dora wrote to Molly and Kirby in Roane County. She explained what she had thought about and asked their opinion.

"I'm so anxious to hear back," confided Dora to her older sister, Stella. They were sitting in her living room having coffee while Stella's twins were napping.

"I've been feeling so well with this baby, Dora. I'm not going to ask you to help out this time, as all of us do. I know it's always, 'Dora, come', and, 'Dora, do this, Dora do that.' You must get very tired of it."

"Well, yes, a little. But it helps when I'm paid well. I've saved up enough to start sewing on a new wardrobe. I need a trunk, and I'm expecting you and Andrew to order me a nice one. For that favor, I will stay with you until I hear from Kirby and Molly."

"It's a deal," said Stella. "I hear Jonathon stirring. He'll wake his brother if I don't get in there."

Rueben and Annabel

Annabel had planned everything out. There seemed to be no real problems. Rueben and she had walked out to spend a few minutes looking over the land. Rueben had been so happy these last few days; he could hardly believe things were moving so quickly. They had stopped at a small stream to get a sip of water, and noticed that there was a little cabin beyond the trees. It looked to be a one-roomed little hut with a chimney; the logs were weathered and silver colored.

"Look," said Annabel. "Let's go closer. Isn't it just a darling little house?"

"Be careful, dear. There may be snakes or other wild things there. Let me cut a stick to carry for protection before we go closer."

As they approached they saw there was a small window in the hut, and Rueben leaned over to look inside.

"It's empty except for a small cot," he said. "I'll go in first with my stick and scare out any varmints."

The door was not locked and Reuben went inside slowly, poking about with the pole. "I guess it's safe. This could be cleaned up and used for a rest place when we work on the property."

"Oh, Rueben. I just love it."

"It's all right," he answered.

They returned the next day. Annabel swept out the little cabin and Rueben cleaned out the tiny fireplace to make sure they could build a safe fire. In a huge apron Annabel was already dusty.

Rube climbed up a rickety ladder to check out the loft. "What a mess," he said. "Birds have been up here. It will take days to get it clean enough to even have some coffee in this place."

"Never mind. You concentrate on building our new house and I'll do my best here. I love this little cabin. Thank goodness they left it; whoever they were. Now let's head on home and see what's for supper."

****

Thelma and Charlie had a letter from Bo. They shared it with Annabel.

Dear Charlie and Thelma,

I have done well so far here. I enclose my address. I have a room in a boarding house and it's quite the thing I need. The owner is a very kind and caring lady, and I have a clean room.

I have found a job in a shoe store that is also a shoe repair shop. The pay is enough to keep me until I find something else. I am really liking being on my own. It's a good feeling. Please write me here. I'm sending a letter off to Mama this weekend. I hope she wasn't too upset at my abrupt leaving. It was really the only way I could do it. I think she and Ben will understand when they get my letter. Tell Rueben hello for me. I'll close now.

Your brother, Bo."

Charlie read it aloud to everyone. Then Annabel wanted to read it for herself. "I left word for Andrew to send my mail here, so I should get my letter in a few days," she announced.

Ben said "Good old Bo. He had to go see the world for himself. I miss him. I'll write a long letter to him immediately."

Lester Dunn

Sam Lawson was out looking for limbs that had been blown down in storms. He knew they would be dry and seasoned and good for starting fires. He saw a man just down the way doing the same thing. He threw out his hand. "Hello. I'm Sam Lawson."

"Lester Dunn. Am I trespassing? I've just come to inspect the property I bought and I'm not sure of the boundaries yet."

"Not at all. It looks like we'll be neighbors. My wife, Amelia, and her two children and I live just over the hill. And my wife is expecting another baby soon. How about you ... do you have family?"

"Yes. My mother, her sister, and I are staying at the inn in town. We want to camp out here as soon as I can get us a shelter ready. It's pretty dense, though. I think there'll be a lot of work ahead of me before I can bring them."

"Well, nice to meet you. Good luck with your property. I'm sure we'll see you again soon."

Amelia

Will and his family had just arrived at church the next Sunday. Nancy and Mike were both dressed in new clothes, as they were growing very quickly now. He helped Lydia and the children climb down from the wagon seat, and was just starting to take the team around and tie them to an oak tree when he was surprised to hear his name called. He turned to see Dr. McDonald enter the church yard. He went to meet the older man.

"Will, I have some very sad news. I've been out to Sam's house all night. Amelia has had a miscarriage. The baby was a boy. Sam is devastated. Will you have the pastor tell everyone at church? I need to go home and get some sleep."

"I'm so sorry to hear that. Of course. Lydia and I will go out there and see them, too."

With a heavy heart Will walked over to talk with Pastor Greene.

The next few days were filled with sorrow for Sam and his family. Amelia stayed in bed and refused to eat. Carrie and Dora tried to coax her, but to no avail. Amelia relived the hours over and over seeing the little blanketed body of her lifeless son. She was unable to attend the funeral because the doctor insisted that she not leave her bed for a week.

The house seemed full of people, bringing ham, baked chicken and other foods, but Amelia yearned to tell them all to stay away and let her grieve in peace.

Sam was heartbroken too, but also worried about his wife. Nothing seemed to help. After awhile, Dora left for home, which left Carrie to do all the housework and cooking.

Sam talked to Kathy. He asked her if she thought Malinda would be interested in coming to spend some time helping Carrie with the house. It seemed unfair to burden Carrie with all the responsibilities of running a house and caring for her mother too. He knew Dora had begun sewing new dresses for herself, and was making plans to leave the mountain. He wouldn't ask her to return and work again.

Malinda was happy to come and help out. She liked the change and could use the money she was offered. She hoped she would even be the one who could persuade Amelia to come out of her bedroom.

Carrie Beal and Lester Dunn

As Carrie went walking one day to get out of the dismal surroundings of her mother's grief, she suddenly saw a bundle of white fur in the brush. She realized she had come away without a gun or any protection and was a bit frightened. Then she saw it was only a little puppy, and she scooped it up. Hearing a man's voice she paused with the small dog still in her arms. A tall man with unruly brown hair rode into the lane. He jumped down from his horse when he saw the pretty young lady holding his dog.

"So you've found my runaway, I see. I'm much obliged to you. My name's Lester Dunn. I've just bought this property." He motioned with his arms outspread.

"I'm glad to meet you. I'm Carrie Beal." She handed the puppy to him. "Our home is up this lane and I was just out for a walk. You must drop in some time and meet my mother, brother and step-father."

"Thanks for the invitation. I believe I may have met your step-father. Is his name Sam Lawson? We were both out here gathering fallen wood from the forest just recently."

He grinned unexpectedly, and Carrie found she couldn't resist smiling broadly in response.

Eventually she recovered her wits, and managed to talk with him about the weather and other small talk.

She walked back to the house deep in thought. "He's sure a handsome man," she thought. "Not a boy like my brother, James, but a grown man." He had mentioned his mother and aunt; she took that to mean that he probably wasn't married. She determined that she would ask Sam to invite this Mr. Dunn to dinner; well, once her mother was feeling better, anyway. Smiling, she continued on her way.

When Carrie entered the door at home she was happy to see that her mother had finally come to the parlor, even though she was still bundled in a robe. She gave her a quick hug, then quickly went into the kitchen to share her news.

"Oh, Malinda. I've just seen the most handsome man ... and he's our new next door neighbor."

Malinda looked up. "Well, good for you. Now will you tell James to fill the wood box? I'll need to heat some water. Your mother has just asked for a cup of tea."

****

Amelia continued to improve, and finally felt well enough to agree to Carrie and Sam's suggestion that they invite Lester for dinner; she even insisted that he bring his mother and aunt along. "We would be glad to have them and I could use the company," she said.

Sam was pleased that Amelia was once again interested in being with other people.

James was especially interested in Lester. He looked ahead and saw that he could possibly get some work there helping clear the Dunn's land.

During the next weeks Lester's mother Maud and his aunt Mamie spent hours with Amelia, sewing, quilting and cooking. The three became great friends.

James got his wish, too; Lester paid him to help chop down trees and burn out stumps.

James took his new friend hunting for game and scouring the woods for herbs and setting traps. He showed him how to add to his bank account by taking what he found and caught to sell to the general store and the local inns.

They built a temporary lean-to for the horses. When rain caught the young men hard at work, the little shed was perfect and they sheltered there, always talking and planning their next project.

"You need to order some chickens, Lester," advised James.

"That's a good idea. I'll put out the word that I'll need a cow soon, also. When I go into town again, I'll see about both."

Lester's Cabin

The wonderful day arrived when the clearing was large enough to start Lester's cabin. Sam declared they would make a picnic of it and packed the wagon. Maud and Mamie had been staying nights with Amelia and Sam, so they were quite excited about the new arrangements.

Logs were lying in piles, drying out for the walls of the new house. Carrie had spread blankets to sit on and Sam had built a fire to heat water to boil coffee.

Everyone was in good spirits. James carried water from the spring and Maud set out food.

"I really like this new neighbor and his folks," commented Will, watching Lester showing his mother where he planned to place their house. "They have determination."

"Yes, it took a lot of courage for Maud and Mamie to come all this way," Lydia agreed. She added, "it's especially rewarding to see Amelia here with her family."

Sam's wife still looked underweight and pale, but it was good for her to be there, surrounded and supported by her old friends ... and her new friends, too.

Maud was sure that Carrie was attracted to her son, but she kept quiet. She liked the young woman and hoped that Lester would return her interest. When she heard him ask Carrie if she wanted to see the shelter and lean to that he and James had built, she watched with delight as Carrie rose and shyly followed him out of sight of the others.

Lester was quite proud to show his friend all he had done, and she was impressed by his accomplishments.

"You have done very well," Carrie told him. "I can't wait to see your house go up. I'll help as much as I can. All this activity has been very good for Mama, too, Lester. She's been grieving for her lost baby, you know."

"I'm glad. It's been a blessing for my mother, too, to have new friends and no time to be homesick."

****

When it was finally time for the roof to go on Lester's house, Andrew put up a notice at the general store in Norma, inviting everyone to attend. It was quite a celebration at the little clearing as many of the Dunn family's new friends made their way there to put on the roof and nail on the split shingles.

Will and Lydia

Will sat with Lydia in the shade of a huge oak, watching the merriment of the Dunn's roof raising celebration.

He remembered back to the day he brought his wife and their four young children from Alabama, returning to his old home in Scott County, and he smiled.

He knew what Lester was feeling and he was glad. He said a silent prayer for him and his family and hoped Scott County would treat the Dunn family as well as it had treated the Wilsons.

Made in the USA
San Bernardino, CA
11 July 2014